The Whole Package

# 餐飲人員說英語
# 邁向國際的
# 必備關鍵

MP3

客訴問題如何處理?會用英文電話訂位嗎?內外場狀況如何應對?
一次搞懂內、外場狀況,即刻解決各式餐飲疑難!

陳怡歆 ◎ 著

✔ 看「餐飲應答篇」,練就三寸不爛之舌,翻轉成「考官」、「面試官」眼中的明日之星!

規劃「一問三答」,由三種答題思路練習,以各種角度回答問題,最後融入自己本身經驗,發展出令口試考官驚豔的答案,於考場中大放異彩。

✔ 精讀「餐飲搶分篇」,懂得改變思維、換位思考你就是「主管」、「老闆」不可或缺的得力助手!

「情境對話」提供即效性口語表達,在各餐飲流程中使用「對」的用語,解決不知如何電話訂位、處理餐間服務等的窘境!「哪裡有問題」讓你具備最正確的心態且了解問題根源,餐飲流程上的各種問題迎刃而解。

# 作者序

餐飲業從來就不是錢多事少的行業，然而，也許是因為我
對美食的熱忱、以及對新鮮事物的好奇心，我無法不喜歡
餐飲業的工作。開啟我對餐飲之路興趣的，是在一家外國
人的餐廳當服務生。當時還對服務生懷抱美好幻想的我，
在上工之後，才發現並非打扮漂亮、待人有禮便能輕鬆完
成任務。之後前往日本工作，對日本人在服務、盤飾、衛
生整潔等細節上的要求感到印象深刻。踏上美國國土後，
更因為完全不同於亞洲風格的餐飲文化，而感到極為震
驚。餐飲業是個博大精深的世界，而不同的文化更有不同
的習慣及講究。要在一個不同的國度中生存，除了自身技
術的磨練外，對該國的文化認識更是不可或缺。希冀讀者
們能在學英文的同時，細細品味不同國家的風土民情，並
體會學習英語的樂趣。

陳怡歆

# 編者序

餐飲英語在各類表達上，其實都不太一樣，對許多習慣國內英語學習方式跟考試方式的學生來說，在與客人外語應答上仍稍嫌不足，語言使用也不夠道地，這次有幸邀請到在台灣、日本和美國，都有餐飲工作經驗的作者來撰寫這本書。

Part1 為一問三答的部分，提供讀者更多元的答題思路，有效提升餐飲口說應答實力。答案部分極為簡短，在面試的短回答上，除了提供即效性跟臨場反應性，更能顯示答題者的充分準備。

Part2 則包含極為簡易的情境對話，當中反應出了實際的餐飲經驗。較少開口說英文者，可以更注意要如何以英文回應客人。此外，每則對話後，規劃了「哪裡有問題」單元，讀者讀了情境對話後，除了學習英文使用外，更該知道情境對話中，是哪裡出了問題，並從中學習。「餐飲補充包」的單元中，更提供了該補強的部分，從中加強自我餐飲實力。

編輯部　敬上

目次
*Contents*

Part

1

餐飲應答篇

## 學習進度表

看完後別忘了打勾喔！

# Reception
# 招呼與帶位

 **一問三答**

For a customer, a **heart-warming greeting** and **reception** are so important. These **determine** the image of the restaurant. Do you have any **tips** to share when it comes to this simple yet **decisive** gesture?

身為一位客人，受到熱情的招呼和接待很重要，這些決定了一家餐廳的形象。你們對於這個簡單卻重要的動作，是否有什麼訣竅可以分享呢？

*Alina* 艾琳娜

Well, I'm not very comfortable with the customers. I mean, I can cook for them, I can run the business, but talking to the customers **face to face** is not ***my cup of tea***. I may have to learn it **eventually**, but **certainly** not for now.

我對接待客人不是很在行。我是說，我可以為他們做餐點，我也可以經營一家店，但跟客人面對面聊天真的非我所長。我終究還是得學這方面，但絕不是現在。

Being **hospitable** is big. No matter how bad you feel, the moment the customers **step through** the **threshold**, you have to put away your **private** feelings and start smiling. It's something against human **nature**, but it's **indispensable**. I can only say that *practice makes perfect*.

熱情待客很重要。不論你的心情多憂鬱，在客人踏進店門的剎那，你必須全部拋諸腦後，並綻出微笑。這是違反人性的事，但非做不可。我只能說熟能生巧。

Allen 艾倫

I'm born to be a server, I feel. I'm always in a good mood and I want to make people feel **cozy** and **laid back**. Just **picture** yourself walking into a restaurant. Would you like to see a **cold stiff face**? No! So that's what I tell myself, and I **nail it** every time.

我覺得我生來就是當服務生的料，我的心情總是很好，而且我想讓人們覺得舒適、放鬆。想像你走進一家餐廳，你會想看到冷冰冰的臉孔嗎？當然不！我都是這麼告訴自己的，而每次我總是做得很成功。

# 字彙和慣用語一覽表

| heart-warming | adj. 令人窩心的 | greeting | n. 招呼 |
|---|---|---|---|
| reception | n. 接待 | determine | v. 決定 |
| tip | n. 秘方；秘訣 | decisive | adj. 決定性的 |
| face to face | 面對面 | eventually | adv. 終究 |
| certainly | adv. 無疑地 | hospitable | adj. 好客 |
| step through | 走過；越過 | threshold | n. 門檻 |
| private | adj. 私人的 | nature | n. 天性 |
| indispensable | adj. 不可或缺的 | cozy | adj. 舒適的 |
| lay back | 放鬆 | picture | v. 想像 |
| nail sth. | 成功做到某事 | cold stiff face | （臉）冷若冰霜 |

# 好好用句型

本書一問三答中出現許多實用的句型或是短句，拿來練習最好不過了，現在也馬上試試看吧！看完之後，馬上就能輕鬆學會，不用背誦！

**句型一 ▶ my cup of tea** 不擅長某事；不合某人品味

**1** **Jane :** Do you want to watch Mr. and Ms. Smith with me?
珍：妳要不要跟我一起看《史密斯夫婦》？

**2** **Laura :** No, thanks. Action movies are not my cup of tea.
蘿拉：不，謝了。我不喜歡動作片。

**句型二 ▶ practice makes perfect** 熟能生巧

**1** **Matt :** Why can't I master the omelet?
麥特：為什麼我的煎蛋捲總是做不好？

**2** **Keith :** Don't you worry. Practice makes perfect.
凱斯：別擔心，熟能生巧。

一問三答

 MP3 02

When a customer asks for a menu **introduction**, do you have any **principles** or **priorities**? Is it the same to start from any **item**, or does it matter?

當客人要你們介紹菜單時,你們是否有什麼原則或順序呢? 介紹餐點的先後順序是否會影響客人的點餐?

 *Alina* 艾琳娜

Absolutely. I always start from the entrées. **Not only** because it's more **profitable** for us, **but also** because every dish is my ***pride and joy***. I love our grilled ribs, meatloaf, pork chops, and burgers. Appetizers and desserts have their reason to **exist**, but they are not my **focus**.

當然了,我總是先從主餐開始介紹。不只是因為主餐收益較高,也因為每道菜都是我的驕傲。我愛我們的烤肋排、肉派、豬排和漢堡。開

胃菜和甜點當然也有存在的必要，但並非我的重點。

Cathy 凱西

The priority does matter. Since there are many items on the menu, it's impossible to introduce every dish, which means that we have to **omit** some items in the introduction. I often start from our **best-sellers**, because everyone has their own **taste**, and the best-sellers **please** most of them.

順序當然有影響，因為菜單上品項很多，不可能一一介紹，因此有些菜不會被介紹到。我總是從銷路最好的料理開始介紹，因為每個人喜好不同，而銷路最好的料理是受到多人喜愛並認可的。

Allen 艾倫

I think the **type** of the customer matters when **presenting** the menu. If it's a group of young people, I **prefer** to start from burgers and beers. If it's a family, I'll **recommend** kid-friendly meals. If it's a couple, they might need something special and **elegant**. For them, pasta dishes and sandwiches won't be *the best choice*.

我想客人的類型會影響在介紹菜單這件事上。如果是一群年輕人，我偏好從漢堡和啤酒開始介紹。如果是家庭用餐，我會推薦兒童也方便食用的餐點。如果是夫妻或情侶，他們會需要一點特殊、可以優雅地吃的餐點，那義大利麵和三明治就不會是首選。

# 字彙和慣用語一覽表

| | | | |
|---|---|---|---|
| introduction | n. 介紹 | principle | n. 原則 |
| priority | n. 優先順序 | item | n. 品項 |
| not only…but also | 不只…還有… | profitable | adj. 有利的、有益的 |
| exist | v. 存在 | focus | n. 焦點 |
| omit | v. 省略 | best-seller | 最熱賣的商品 |
| taste | n. 喜好 | please | v. 取悅 |
| type | n. 類型；樣式 | present | v. 展示 |
| prefer | v. 偏愛 | recommend | v. 推薦 |
| elegant | adj. 優雅的 | | |

補充字彙

| | | | |
|---|---|---|---|
| neglect | v. 省略 | kind | n. 種類；類型 |
| emphasis | n. 強調 | | |

# 好好用句型

本書一問三答中出現許多實用的句型或是短句，拿來練習最好不過了，現在也馬上試試看吧！看完之後，馬上就能輕鬆學會，不用背誦！

句型一 ▶ **pride and joy** 引以為傲的人事物

1 **Lauren :** Your daughter is such a shining star!
羅倫：妳的女兒真是顆閃耀之星呢！

2 **Mason :** Yeah, she is my pride and joy.
梅森：可不是嗎，她是我的驕傲。

句型二 ▶ **the best choice** 首選；聰明的選擇

1 **Kelly :** I think I should call in sick, so I can go out with Jason.
凱利：我應該請病假，這樣才能跟傑森去約會。

2 **April :** I don't think that's the best choice you can make.
艾芙蘿：我不認為這是明智之舉。

# Orders
# 點餐

## 一問三答

What is the most important thing when it comes to ordering? Do you have any **incredible errors** to talk about?

點餐時該注意的要點是什麼呢？你們能分享一些難以置信的失誤嗎？

Alina 艾琳娜

I mentioned before that I'm not good at **dealing with** the guests, and that's because I **mistook** their orders before. It's pretty **frustrating** when people require their food in a certain way, and you **fail to memorize** it all. Note taking is definitely **essential**, but even so I can't **assure** that everything **goes smooth**.

我早先提過我不是很會跟客人周旋，那是因為我有一次誤點了客人的

餐。當客人對他們的餐點有些特殊要求，而你沒辦法記住全部的細節時，真的很令人挫敗。點餐一定要筆記，但就算如此，我也無法保證事事順利。

*Cathy* 凱西

You will need a **note pad** with you while taking orders. For instance, if someone wants meatloaf without ketchup and another wants **extra** caramelized onions, things might get **confused** easily. I haven't made a huge mistake yet, but you never know what will happen. ***There's no such thing*** as being **overly** prepared.

點餐時，你會需要一本小記事本。舉例來說，如果有人點了肉派不加番茄醬，另一個人點肉派和特多焦糖洋蔥，這很容易搞混。我還沒犯過嚴重大錯，但你永遠不知道未來會發生什麼事。多做點準備總是好的。

*Allen* 艾倫

I once brought a plate of hash browns with **Hungarian** meat sauce instead of cream of mushroom to a customer. For her, it was a big problem because she was a vegetarian, and I **guaranteed** her that we had a vegan hash brown **combo**. It was a **catastrophe**. Since then, I take extra **caution** while taking orders.

19

有一次，我本應給客人蘑菇白醬炸薯餅，卻拿成匈牙利肉醬炸薯餅。對她來說，這是個很大的冒犯，因為她是素食主義者，而我向她保證我們提供素食炸薯餅套餐。那是個災難。自從那次起，我總是在點餐時格外留心。

 ## 字彙和慣用語一覽表

| incredible | adj. 荒謬的 | error | n. 錯誤 |
|---|---|---|---|
| deal with | 處理… | mistake | v. 誤會；弄錯 |
| frustrating | adj. 令人受挫的 | fail to | 做…失敗 |
| memorize | v. 記憶 | essential | adj. 必要的 |
| assure | v. 保證 | note pad | n. 隨身小冊子 |
| extra | adj. 額外的 | confused | adj. 混淆的 |
| overly | adv. 過度地 | Hungarian | adj. 匈牙利的 |
| guarantee | v. 保證 | combo | n. 套餐 |
| catastrophe | n. 大災難 | caution | n. 注意 |

補充字彙

| muddled | adj. 含糊的 | vigilance | n. 警覺心 |
|---|---|---|---|

# 好好用句型

本書一問三答中出現許多實用的句型或是短句，拿來練習最好不過了，現在也馬上試試看吧！看完之後，馬上就能輕鬆學會，不用背誦！

句型一 ▶ **go smooth** 順利進行

**1** **Lizzie :** Are you sure that this trick is gonna work?
莉茲：妳確定這招行得通嗎？

**2** **Karen :** No worries. Things will surely go smooth.
凱倫：別擔心，事情一定會順利進行的。

句型二 ▶ **there's no such thing** 沒有…的事

**1** **Zoe :** There's no such thing of having too much ice cream.
奏伊：冰淇淋永遠不嫌多。

**2** **Larry :** Hey, watch your belly!
賴瑞：小心妳的小腹越來越大。

# Serving
# 上餐

Serving seems to be the easiest thing in the whole meal service. Is it true? Why, or why not?

上餐感覺好像是整個餐飲服務過程中最簡單的事。是否屬實？為什麼簡單，或為什麼不呢？

Alina 艾琳娜

Being **attentive** and **prudent** is **crucial** when it comes to serving the meal. It's not just bringing the food to the customer, but also **a chance to** show that you want the customers to enjoy what is on the plate. Therefore, a warm smile and **delightful** voice is what should **accompany** the food to the table.

送餐時，務必保持警覺，行動謹慎，這非常重要。這不只是將食物送到客人那兒而已，更是展現你希望顧客好好享受盤中飧的機會。因此，一抹溫暖的微笑，愉悅的聲音都必須伴隨著美食上桌。

Cathy 凱西

For me, serving the food is **literally** the easiest part. What is **troublesome** is the **complaints** that might come after it. Being **smiley** and **positive** while serving the food that we **are proud of** is human **instinct**, facing the complaints isn't so natural. Taking some of the **irrational** complaints is *the last thing* I usually want to do.

對我來說，送餐真的如字面上的簡單，麻煩的是隨之而來的客訴。帶著微笑、殷勤地供應我們引以為傲的餐點，這是身為人的直覺，但處理客訴卻非如此。對付某些不合理的抱怨真是我最不想面對的事。

Allen 艾倫

I still *jump up on my toes* when I hear the kitchen **cry out** "order up". It's like magic words that make me **instantly** run in there to take the food. It's an **exciting** moment when the food is **piping hot**, smelling heavenly, and ready to be delivered to the **empty** stomachs waiting for it. I don't know if I'll ever **get tired of** it.

直到現在，當廚房大喊「上菜！」時，我還是會立刻跳起來。那些字眼就像魔法般帶著我即刻衝進廚房拿餐點。餐點熱騰騰、香氣四溢、準備被送進空洞的胃袋的時刻很讓人興奮。我覺得我永不會對這項工作感到厭煩。

# 字彙和慣用語一覽表

| attentive | adj. 細心的 | prudent | adj. 謹慎的 |
|---|---|---|---|
| crucial | adj. 關鍵的 | a chance to | 從事…的機會 |
| delightful | adj. 令人愉悅的 | accompany | v. 陪伴 |
| literally | adv. 字面上地 | troublesome | adj. 棘手的 |
| complaint | n. 抱怨 | smiley | adj. 笑容滿面的 |
| positive | adj. 正向的 | be proud of | 以…為榮 |
| instinct | n. 直覺 | irrational | adj. 無理的 |
| cry out | 大喊；大叫 | instantly | adv. 立即地 |
| exciting | adj. 令人興奮的 | piping hot | 熱氣蒸騰的 |
| empty | adj. 空洞的 | get tired of | 對…感到厭倦 |

# 好好用句型

本書一問三答中出現許多實用的句型或是短句，拿來練習最好不過了，現在也馬上試試看吧！看完之後，馬上就能輕鬆學會，不用背誦！

**句型一 ▶ the last thing** 最不想做（的事）

**1** **Catherine :** Doing the final essay is the last thing I want to do.
凱瑟琳：期末報告是我最不想做的事。

**2** **Barbara :** Me too. Well, you gotta do what you gotta do.
芭芭拉：我也是，但該做的事還是得做。

**句型二 ▶ jump up on one's toe** （嚇到）跳起來

**1** **Jim :** Surprise!
吉姆：驚喜！

**2** **Bobby :** You almost make me jump up on my toe, man!
鮑比：你差點嚇死我耶，老兄！

# Service during Meal
# 餐間服務

 **Q&A** 一問三答

Being a server is an art. It truly isn't *as easy as it sounds*. Do you have any tips to share for being a perfect server?

當服務生是門藝術，不如聽起來簡單。你們是否有任何當完美服務生的秘訣呢？

*Alina* 艾琳娜

Every **skill** needs to be **trained**, so does being a server. If one is **unfamiliar** with serving people, no doubt one is going to have a hard time. **Keen observation** is **fundamental**; diligence and **hospitality** are also top priorities. Never **be afraid to communicate**. **Unless** one faces the problem, it can't be **coped with**.

凡事都需要訓練，當服務生也一樣。如果一個人對服務別人不熟悉，不用說，他會過得很辛苦。敏銳的觀察是最基本的，勤奮和好客的態

度也很重要。永遠不要擔心和人溝通，除非你正視問題，否則無法解決問題。

Cathy 凱西

I've seen bad servers. Being a server or a floor manager doesn't mean **harassing** the guests **unceasingly**. There was one guy that kept talking to the customers and causing them to leave earlier. This isn't caring for the customers; it's **feeding his own ego**.

我看過很糟糕的服務生，身為服務生或經理並不代表要一直騷擾客人。曾有一位服務生不斷跟客人攀談，結果導致客人提早離席。他不是在關照客人，而是在滿足自己的虛榮心。

Allen 艾倫

The **knack** is to enjoy what you do. Try to ***think in other people's shoes***. When serving our diners, I want them to have the best dining experience possible. That is so important. Refilling the water, changing tableware, providing **napkins**, these are just the basics. Don't **go by the book**. Be human, be friendly, and the customers will notice that.

訣竅在於你樂於所做的，試著用同理心去對待別人。當我在服務客人時，我希望他們能擁有最棒的用餐經驗。所以添水、換餐具、提供餐巾等只是最基本的服務。不要死板的照本宣科，要像人、像一位朋友，這樣客人自然會注意到。

## 字彙和慣用語一覽表

| | | | |
|---|---|---|---|
| skill | n. 技術；技巧 | train | v. 訓練 |
| unfamiliar | adj. 不熟悉的 | keen | adj. 敏銳的 |
| observation | n. 觀察；觀察力 | fundamental | adj. 基本的 |
| hospitality | n. 好客 | be afraid to | 害怕做… |
| communicate | v. 溝通 | unless | adv. 除非 |
| cope with | 處理；應付 | harass | v. 騷擾 |
| unceasingly | adv. 不間斷的 | feed one's ego | 使人感覺良好 |
| knack | n. 技巧；竅門 | napkin | n. 餐巾 |
| go by the book | 照本宣科 | | |

補充字彙

| | | | |
|---|---|---|---|
| unacquainted | adj. 陌生的 | bother | v. 打擾 |
| friendliness | n. 親善；和睦 | | |

 ## 好好用句型

本書一問三答中出現許多實用的句型或是短句，拿來練習最好不過了，現在也馬上試試看吧！看完之後，馬上就能輕鬆學會，不用背誦！

**句型一 ▶ as easy as it sounds** 如聽起來一般簡單（常用否定）

**①** **Betty :** Cooking a main course in thirty minutes is a piece of cake.

貝蒂：在三十分鐘內做出一道主菜是輕而易舉的事。

**②** **Rick :** I don't think so. It is not as easy as it sounds.

瑞奇：我可不這麼想，這沒有聽起來那樣簡單。

**句型二 ▶ think in other people's shoes** 設身處地為人設想；有同理心

**①** **Fanny :** Removing all the shells of the shrimps is such an unnecessary work!

芳妮：幫所有的蝦子剝殼真是不必要的差事！

**②** **Melissa :** Think in other people's shoes. You don't want to have shell-on shrimps in your pasta, do you?

梅麗莎：有點同理心吧，妳希望自己義大利麵裡的蝦子是帶殼的嗎？

# 2.1 Reservations
## 訂位

It's always exciting to have people call in for reservations. What's important while taking phone calls like this?

有人打電話訂位總是件令人興奮的事。接訂位電話時,什麼事需要注意呢?

*Alina* 艾琳娜

It's **obligatory** to take the customer's name, number, and the **amount** of guests. Sometimes, there are groups of twelve or groups of twenty people wanting reservations. When that happens, we may have to **rearrange** the dining **area** to ***fit in*** such a big group.

務必留下客人的姓名、電話號碼,及來店人數。有時候會有十二或二

十人的團體預約，這時候我們就必須重新安排用餐區的座位配置，好容納這麼多人。

Cathy 凱西

As Alina said, we often have to rearrange the dining area for big groups, so we'd better make sure that our guests arrive **on time**. If the guests don't **show up** at the **scheduled** hour, we have a ten-minute **policy** of **holding** their seats **open**. No longer than that.

就像艾琳娜說的，我們必須為團體預約重新排位子，所以最好確保他們在預約的時間抵達。如果客人沒有依約定的時間出現，我們有留位十分鐘的策略，時間超過就不再保留了。

Allen 艾倫

Name and phone number are the **basic** requirements for these **occasions**. The groups often have **expectations** for certain seats, such as a four-person family wanting a corner table or a two-person group wanting sofa seats. Our job is to make sure that things are **arranged** properly **ahead of** time.

客人的姓名和電話號碼是訂位時最基本的資訊。通常客人都會自己選定座位，例如四人小家庭想要沙發座而情侶兩人就想要角落的桌次。我們的工作就是確保事情能提前妥善安排。

# 字彙和慣用語一覽表

| | | | |
|---|---|---|---|
| obligatory | adj. 必須的 | amount | n. 數量 |
| rearrange | v. 重新配置 | area | n. 區域 |
| on time | 準時 | show up | 現身 |
| scheduled | adj. 表定的 | policy | n. 政策 |
| hold open | （座位）開放 | basic | adj. 基本的 |
| occasion | n. 場合；時機 | expectation | n. 期許；期待 |
| arrange | v. 安排；布置 | ahead of | 在…之前 |

補充字彙

| | | | |
|---|---|---|---|
| on the phone | 電話中 | in person | 親自 |
| show off | 炫耀 | circumstance | n. 情境；情況 |
| optional | adj. 選擇性的 | in time | 及時 |

# 好好用句型

本書一問三答中出現許多實用的句型或是短句，拿來練習最好不過了，現在也馬上試試看吧！看完之後，馬上就能輕鬆學會，不用背誦！

**句型一 ▶ fit in** （人）融入環境；使適合

1. **Sunny :** I'm so nervous. What if your family doesn't like me?

   珊妮：我好緊張，如果你的家人不喜歡我怎麼辦？

2. **Jack :** Don't be silly. You'll fit right in.

   傑克：別傻了，他們一定會愛死妳的。

**補充句型 ▶ get the job done** 把事情做好

1. **Miley :** I really don't want to do this filthy job.

   麥莉：我真不想做這骯髒的差事。

2. **Selena :** Stop complaining. Just get the job done.

   席琳娜：少抱怨了，快把事情做完吧。

# Pickup Orders
# 外帶點餐

**Q&A** 一問三答

MP3 07

Do you offer pickup order service? What is to **be noted** when dealing with a pickup order?

你們是否提供外帶點餐呢？什麼是外帶點餐該注意的事項？

*Alina* 艾琳娜

Pickup ordering is big business and it's popular among **folks**. I was afraid of **hoax** calls but things have ***turned out to be*** great so far. It's very important to take the customer's phone number and give a proper **estimate** to the customer about when the food will be ready.

外帶點餐是個很大的商機，人們也喜歡。我本來很擔心會有惡作劇點餐電話，但到目前為止還沒發生過。留下客人的電話號碼，並告知正確的等待時間很重要。

*Cathy* 凱西

I like the idea of pickup orders a lot. It's convenient for both us and the guests. Usually, the takeout box is **sealed *in the last minutes*** of preparing an order to **prevent** the **loss** of certain **textures** in the food. I don't want the guest picking up our fried chicken and it's **soggy** already.

我很喜歡外帶點餐的點子，這對我們和客人都很方便。通常外帶盒是在最後一刻才密封，這樣能避免一些食材喪失口感。我可不想要客人外帶炸雞，卻發現麵衣已經濕軟了。

*Allen* 艾倫

You have to give the right amount of pickup time; not too long, not too short. Being familiar with every dish will help you with this. **On average**, a pickup order takes about 25 minutes. You want to help the customers arrive on time so the food is fresh and hot.

你必須告知正確的等待時間，不能太長，也不能太短。對每道料理熟悉能幫助你掌握正確時間。平均而言，外帶點餐須等二十五分鐘。你會希望客人抵達的時候食物剛好做好，還是熱騰騰的。

# 字彙和慣用語一覽表

| be noted | 留心；注意 | folks | n. 眾人 |
|---|---|---|---|
| hoax | n. 惡作劇 | estimate | v. 估計 |
| seal | v. 密封 | prevent | v. 預防；防止 |
| loss | n. 損失 | texture | n. 質地 |
| soggy | adj. 軟爛的 | on average | 平均而言 |

補充字彙

| mention | v. 提起；說到 | prank | n. 騙局 |
|---|---|---|---|
| approximate | adj. 大約的 | roughly | adv. 粗略地 |
| mushy | adj. 糊狀的 | dull | adj. 乏味的 |
| grainy | adj. 顆粒感的 | messy | adj. 髒兮兮的 |
| impatient | adj. 不耐煩的 | anxiously | adj. 焦躁的 |

# 好好用句型

本書一問三答中出現許多實用的句型或是短句，拿來練習最好不過了，現在也馬上試試看吧！看完之後，馬上就能輕鬆學會，不用背誦！

句型一 ▶ **turn out to be** 結果是…

**1** **Mike :** My proposal turned out to be a disaster. Mary was not surprised at all.

麥克：我的求婚過程真是場災難，瑪莉完全沒有被驚喜到。

**2** **Jacky :** But she said yes, didn't she?

賈姬：但她點頭了，不是嗎？

句型二 ▶ **in the last minute** 在最後一刻

**1** **Ryan :** It's the last day of summer vacation and my assignment is not done yet!

萊恩：暑假最後一天了，我的作業卻還沒寫完！

**2** **Tina :** You always like to do it in the last minute.

蒂娜：你總是拖到最後一刻。

# 2.3 Order Ahead
## 預先點餐

Do you allow the customers to call in and order on the phone? Does it make the serving **process smoother**?

你們允許客人在電話中點餐嗎？這是否讓送餐過程更順暢？

*Alina* 艾琳娜

I never think it's a good idea to let the customers order on the phone. First of all, who knows if they will **cancel** at the last minute? **Secondly**, even if they come as promised, there's a **possibility** that they will change their order when they see the menu. ***In short***, I ***don't care to*** **tackle** the problem.

我從不認為讓客人在電話中點餐是個好點子。首先，誰知道他們會不會在最後一分鐘取消呢？再者，就算他們在預定的時間到來，他們也

可能在看到菜單的時候改變點餐。總之，我可不想處理這些麻煩事。

Cathy 凱西

Normally, I won't **recommend** that, except if it's for **loyal** customers. There are always some faces that you **recognize** and you can put **trust** in them. Other than that, I won't offer taking orders on the phone, unless I am willing to accept responsibility.

通常，我不會建議客人這麼做，除非他們是常客。有些熟面孔你認得，而你信任他們。除此之外，我不會主動請客人在電話中點餐，除非我願意承擔後果。

Allen 艾倫

Well, I don't see it as such a bad thing. If the customer is taking **seniors** or young children with them, they might want to **shorten** the waiting time. I understand it, so sometimes I'd tell them that they can order on the phone. My bosses don't **quite** like it, though.

我覺得這不是件壞事。如果客人有長者或孩子同行，他們可能不想等那麼久。我了解這點，所以有時候我會告訴他們，可以在電話中直接點餐。我的老闆們不喜歡我這麼做就是了。

# 字彙和慣用語一覽表

| | | | |
|---|---|---|---|
| process | n. 過程 | smooth | adj. 順暢的 |
| cancel | v. 取消 | secondly | adv. 再者 |
| possibility | n. 可能性 | tackle | v. 處理 |
| recommend | v. 推薦 | loyal | adj. 忠實的 |
| recognize | v. 認出；認可 | trust | n. 信任 |
| senior | n. 年長者 | shorten | v. 縮短 |
| quite | adv. 十分地 | | |

補充字彙

| | | | |
|---|---|---|---|
| annul | v. 取消 | confrontation | n. 衝突 |
| endorse | v. 支持；贊同 | trustworthy | adj. 值得信任的 |
| reliance | n. 信賴 | reduce | v. 減少；縮小 |
| relatively | adv. 相對地 | | |

# 好好用句型

本書一問三答中出現許多實用的句型或是短句，拿來練習最好不過了，現在也馬上試試看吧！看完之後，馬上就能輕鬆學會，不用背誦！

**句型一 ▶ in short** 簡而言之

**1 Kenny :** It's a long story. I fell in love with another girl, but I couldn't give up on Nancy, so I went out with them both at the same time…

肯尼：說來話長。我愛上了另一個女孩，但我沒辦法放棄南茜，所以我同時跟兩個女孩約會…

**2 Ryan :** In short, Nancy discovered it and she dumped you.

羅恩：總之，南茜後來發現了，並把你給甩了。

**句型二 ▶ don't care to** 不想…

**1 Tammy :** What do you want for lunch? We can have fried rice, or ramen, or dumplings…

泰咪：你午餐想吃什麼？我們可以吃炒飯、拉麵或水餃…

**2 Drake :** I really don't care to think. Let's just have pizza delivery.

德瑞克：我懶得想那麼多，我們叫披薩外送吧。

**一問三答**

MP3
09

If a customer asks for a customized meal on the phone, will you accept it? Does it matter if you **turn** the customer **down**?

如果客人在電話中要求客製化餐點，你們會接受嗎？如果你們拒絕客人的要求，是否會造成什麼影響呢？

 *Alina* 艾琳娜

It depends on the customer. Some people are pretty **stubborn**, but we have to **hold on to** our **quality** and **value**. I do my best to please every customer, so we **discuss** it *back and forth*. This is what is good about the phone: we can discuss and decide. I'd like to produce something fresh and good that our customer can enjoy.

這要看客人方面。有些人很頑固，但我們也必須堅守自己的品質和價

值。我盡量去滿足每位顧客，所以我們會你來我往地討論。這是電話的好處，我們可以商談後再做決定。我很樂意料理新鮮又美味的食物，客人也可以放心享用。

Cathy 凱西

If I'm able to, I surely will. Most of the customers are polite and **considerate**. They don't get upset if their needs are rejected. Instead, they feel sorry about it. **Removing** eggs, dairy and nuts isn't a big thing to me, and that's pretty much what they want most of the time.

能力所及的話，我當然會接受。大多數的客人都有禮且體貼，他們不會因自己的要求被拒而惱羞成怒。相反的，他們會覺得不好意思。不要雞蛋、奶製品和堅果對我來說輕而易舉，而多數時候客人的要求就是這些而已。

Allen 艾倫

Because the kitchen isn't my **territory**, basically I have to depend on Cathy or Alina's decisions. I think when coping with the customers' special needs, thinking in their shoes is the way. I want them to feel **respected**, even on a phone call. The **tone** that you speak to the customer with *matters* a lot.

因為廚房非我所管，所以基本上我聽從凱西和艾琳娜的決策。我認為在處理客人的特殊需求時，應該將心比心。我希望他們覺得自己受到尊重，儘管只是通電話。跟客人說話的語氣非常重要。

# 字彙和慣用語一覽表

| turn sb. down | 拒絕某人 | stubborn | adj. 頑固的 |
|---|---|---|---|
| hold on to | 堅持某事 | quality | n. 品質 |
| value | n. 價值 | discuss | v. 討論 |
| considerate | adj. 體貼的 | remove | v. 移除 |
| territory | n. 領土 | respect | v. 尊重 |
| tone | n. 語氣 | | |
| 補充字彙 | | | |
| inflexible | adj. 死板的 | quantity | n. 數量 |
| valuable | adj. 貴重的 | discussion | n. 討論 |
| talk over sth. | 商討某事 | sympathetic | adj. 有同情心的 |
| eliminate | v. 消除 | self esteem | n. 自尊心 |
| revere | v. 景仰 | | |

# 好好用句型

本書一問三答中出現許多實用的句型或是短句，拿來練習最好不過了，現在也馬上試試看吧！看完之後，馬上就能輕鬆學會，不用背誦！

**句型一 ▶ back and forth** 來回往返

**1 Martin :** Who are you mailing back and forth to?
馬丁：你到底在跟誰魚雁往返呀？

**2 Joey :** It's my girlfriend of course.
喬伊：當然是我的女朋友。

**句型二 ▶ sth. matters** （事）很重要

**1 Grace :** I can't believe that you spent 300 dollars on a pair of glasses.
葛蕾斯：我真不敢相信你花了三百美元買一副眼鏡。

**2 Ian :** Appearance matters.
伊恩：外表很重要。

# 3.1 Opening Hours
# 營業時間

## Q&A 一問三答

Some restaurants don't mind to keep their guests around longer. What's your **opinion** on business hours? Should they be **flexible** or **strict**?

有些餐廳不介意讓客人久留，你們怎麼看營業時間呢？是否要彈性點，還是要嚴格限制？

**Alina 艾琳娜**

I will **leave some room for** negotiation. For instance, if there is a football game going on, I will let the **enthusiastic** guests stay as long as the game goes on. Closing the door on time is **ideal**, but **technically** speaking, this idea doesn't always bring in more profits.

我認為這有討論的空間。舉例來說，如果當天有橄欖球賽，我會讓那

些激昂的客人們待到比賽結束。準時關店雖然理想，但以技術層面來說，這個概念無法帶來更多收益。

**Frankly**, since I'm not the owner, I'd rather **get off duty** on time, although this never happens. Working in a restaurant, you always have extra work to do. Sometimes we even receive orders when we're about to close. All these pots and pans are ***killing me***.

坦白說，因為我不是老闆，我寧可準時下班，雖然這種事從來不會發生。在餐廳工作永遠有做不完的事，有時候我們甚至在關店前收到顧客點餐。清洗這些鍋碗瓢盆真是累壞我了。

Strict business hours are much better for employees. In fact, it's better for everyone **except** the customers. Yet the bosses have different **thinking**. Closing one hour later than business hour is a daily **despair**. If I can only get a day to go home on time. I dare not even think about it.

嚴格規定營業時間對員工來說比較好。事實上，對每個人都比較好，顧客除外；但老闆通常有不一樣的想法。每天幾乎都晚一小時下班，真是令人絕望。希望我有一天能準時回家，這我連想都不敢想。

# 字彙和慣用語一覽表

| | | | |
|---|---|---|---|
| opinion | n. 想法；意見 | flexible | adj. 彈性的 |
| strict | adj. 嚴格的 | negotiation | n. 商討 |
| enthusiastic | adj. 熱情的 | ideal | adj. 理想的 |
| technically | adv. 技術上地 | frankly | adv. 坦白地 |
| get off duty | 下班 | except | 除了…之外 |
| thinking | n. 想法；思考 | despair | n. 絕望 |
| 補充字彙 | | | |
| sb's point of view | 某人的觀點看來 | adaptable | adj. 可通融的 |
| open-minded | adj. 觀念開放的 | severe | adj. 嚴格苛刻的 |
| assumption | n. 假設 | passionate | adj. 對…熱情的 |
| honestly | adv. 誠實地 | excluding | 除…之外 |

# 好好用句型

本書一問三答中出現許多實用的句型或是短句，拿來練習最好不過了，現在也馬上試試看吧！看完之後，馬上就能輕鬆學會，不用背誦！

---

**句型一** ▶ **leave some room for** 有⋯的空間

**1** **Terry :** Are you done?
泰瑞：妳吃飽了嗎？

**2** **Eunice :** Yeah. Just leaving some room for dessert.
優妮絲：差不多了，我還留了空間要吃甜點。

**句型二** ▶ **sth. is killing sb.** 某事使人難受

**1** **Robert :** Lizzy is killing me! She just won't reply my message.
羅伯特：莉婕讓我如坐針氈，她都不回覆我的訊息。

**2** **Varner :** Why don't you call her directly?
瓦勒：何不直接打給她？

# 3.2 Vegetarian Meals
# 是否有素食餐點

## Q&A 一問三答

Do you think that it's **necessary** for a restaurant to **offer** a vegetarian meal? Do you **support** the customers who ask for vegan meals?

你們認為一間餐廳是否有必要提供素食餐點呢？若是客人要求全素餐，你們是否願意配合？

Alina 艾琳娜

Vegetarianism is a **growing trend**. A **successful** restaurant must have vegetarian meals. In my place, I train the staff to talk to our diners as much as possible, so we can understand their needs and offer proper food. Actually, we have a new vegan menu ***on the way***.

素食族群是個成長中的趨勢，一間成功的餐廳必須提供素食餐點。在

我的店裡，我訓練員工盡量多跟客人溝通，了解他們的需求，我們才能提供合適的餐點。實際上，我們正在規畫一份素食菜單。

Cathy 凱西

It's not impossible to make a vegan meal **out of** an ordinary dish. The problem is if we are asked to **modify** our recipes, the texture of the food might not be the same. We always want our guests to understand this, and understand that we are **willing** to **provide** what they want.

將一般料理轉變為素食料理並非不可能，問題在於，當我們被要求更動食譜時，料理的口感可能會變得不一樣。我們總是盡力讓客人了解這點，並讓他們知道我們很樂意調製他們想要的餐點。

Allen 艾倫

I would say one out of ten people might ask for a vegan meal. Based on this, I do *consider* the vegan diet important. We **aim to** give our customers the biggest **satisfaction** we can, so this part really needs to be taken into **consideration**. I usually talk to our customers and bring their needs in the kitchen.

十個人中就有一個人要求素餐，根據這項事實，我的確認為素食餐點很重要。我們致力於給顧客最大的滿足，所以這部分實在需要列入考慮。我總是跟客人談過後，將他們的需求傳達給廚房。

# 字彙和慣用語一覽表

| | | | |
|---|---|---|---|
| necessary | adj. 必要的 | offer | v. 供應 |
| support | v. 支持 | growing | adj. 成長中的 |
| trend | n. 潮流；趨勢 | successful | adj. 成功的 |
| out of | 從…而來 | modify | v. 修改；更動 |
| willing | adj. 樂意的 | provide | v. 提供 |
| aim to | 旨在… | satisfaction | n. 滿意 |
| consideration | n. 考量 | | |

補充字彙

| | | | |
|---|---|---|---|
| increasing | adj. 增加中的 | fashion | n. 潮流；流行 |
| adjust | v. 調整 | adapt to | v. 適應 |
| deliver | v. 提供；遞送 | aim for | 鎖定 |
| thoughtful | adj. 體貼的 | | |

# 好好用句型

本書一問三答中出現許多實用的句型或是短句，拿來練習最好不過了，現在也馬上試試看吧！看完之後，馬上就能輕鬆學會，不用背誦！

句型一 ▶ **on the way** （某事）進行中；（小孩）快出生

**1** **Joseph :** My daughter is on the way. We are so excited!
約瑟：我女兒快出生了，我們都很興奮。

**2** **Kim :** Congrats!
金：恭喜呀！

句型二 ▶ **consider A B** 認為 A 如何

**1** **Jenny :** What do you think of David?
珍妮：妳認為大衛怎麼樣？

**2** **Rita :** I consider him a brave, honest man.
瑞塔：我覺得他是個勇敢又正直的人。

# 3.3 Pet-friendly
## 可以攜帶寵物嗎

**Q&A 一問三答**

MP3 12

---

More and more people keep pets as their family and friends, and some **insist** to bring these "family members" together for a meal. Do you agree on pets' being allowed into your restaurant?

越來越多的人將寵物當作家人及好友，有些人還堅持要帶這些「家族成員」一起用餐。你們同意帶寵物進餐廳嗎？

*Alina* 艾琳娜

It's **ridiculous** to have pets in a food place. Just try to picture the **barking**, the **fur** flying in the air, and all the **hide-and-seek** that these *little fuzzy things* will play. It's not like that I hate animals; I love them, but not in a restaurant! I hope you *get me* on this point.

在吃飯的地方有寵物是一件荒唐的事。想想看狗狗吠叫、動物毛亂飛、還有那些毛小孩會玩的捉迷藏。不是我討厭動物；我喜歡動物，

但餐廳不適合。希望你懂我在說什麼。

Cathy 凱西

Animals are not **suitable** in our diner or in most diners. It's a matter of food **sanitation**. **Suppose that** some dogs and cats have not been **vaccinated**? **Moreover**, if we accept cats and dogs, should we accept birds, frogs, goats, and snakes?

寵物跟我們餐廳格格不入，或許對大部分餐廳都是如此。這是食安問題。若是有些貓狗沒有預防注射怎麼辦？再說，如果我們接納貓狗，我們是不是也要接納鳥、青蛙、山羊和蛇？

Allen 艾倫

Some people do feel it as a loss that their pets are **rejected** everywhere, when they just want to find a **peaceful** place to have a meal. I can understand that feeling. However, according to our **interior** arrangement, it's not a pet-friendly environment. If we were pet-friendly, we may cause human guests and **staff inconvenience**.

有些帶寵物人的確會在到處碰壁後覺得茫然若失，而他們只不過是想安靜地享用一頓飯。我了解那種感受。然而，看看我們的室內擺設，就知道不是個寵物友善的環境。如果我們對寵物友善，可能就會造成其他客人和工作人員的不方便了。

# 字彙和慣用語一覽表

| | | | |
|---|---|---|---|
| insist | v. 堅持 | ridiculous | adj. 荒唐的 |
| bark | v. 吠叫 | fur | n.（動物的）毛 |
| hide-and-seek | 躲貓貓；捉迷藏 | suitable | adj. 合適的 |
| sanitation | n. 衛生 | supposed that | 假如… |
| vaccinate | v. 注射疫苗 | moreover | adv. 再者 |
| reject | v. 拒絕 | peaceful | adj. 安靜的 |
| interior | adj. 內部的 | staff | n. 工作人員 |
| inconvenience | n. 不便 | | |

| 補充字彙 | | | |
|---|---|---|---|
| fuzzy | adj. 毛茸茸的 | dilemma | n. 兩難 |
| serene | adj. 恬靜的 | bug | v. 打擾；使麻煩 |
| refuse | v. 拒絕 | | |

# 好好用句型

本書一問三答中出現許多實用的句型或是短句，拿來練習最好不過了，現在也馬上試試看吧！看完之後，馬上就能輕鬆學會，不用背誦！

**句型一 ▶ little fuzzy things** 泛指貓狗

1 **Taylor :** It's so nice to have these little fuzzy things running around.
泰勒：有這些狗狗在身邊跑來跑去真不錯。

2 **Richard :** Yeah, especially on a cold winter day.
理查：是呀，尤其是在寒冷的冬日裡。

**句型二 ▶ get someone on this point** 懂某人在說什麼

1 **Derek :** Molly can't keep cheating on me! This is the last time!
德瑞克：莫莉不可以再劈腿了！這是最後一次！

2 **Paul :** I get you on this point. You should break up with her.
保羅：我懂你在說什麼。你應該跟她分手才對。

## Q&A 一問三答

In a family-style diner, it is a sure thing that kids often **come along** with their parents. What do you think about serving kids and even infants?

在家庭式的餐館，父母帶孩子前去用餐是很理所當然的事。你們對服務兒童或嬰兒有什麼想法？

Alina 艾琳娜

I'm a mom myself, so I'm **all for** a family to **dine** in my restaurant. Kids are **unpredictable**, they are like **bombs** that will **ignite** when you **least** expect it. For this reason, we have a whole set of kid's tableware and infant chairs. It's a joy to see families dining together, and it's our **duty** to provide a **convivial ambience**.

我自己是個母親，所以我非常贊成一家子到我的餐廳用餐。孩子們很

難控制，他們就像炸彈一樣，會在你沒有警覺的時候引爆。為這緣故，我們購置了整套的兒童餐具以及嬰兒座椅。看家人在一起用餐令人快樂，而我們的責任就是提供一個歡樂的用餐氣氛。

Cathy 凱西

Preparing meals for kids is fun. We have a kid's menu, and it's **basically** everything that adults get but in smaller sizes. We have received **praise** for this and we treat kids like adults. They **deserve** to taste **bold** flavors when they are still young.

準備兒童餐很有趣。我們有兒童菜單，基本上，大人能吃的食物都有，只是分量縮小了一點。不少人稱讚我們的兒童菜單，因為我們把小孩當大人看待。他們值得在小時候就嚐到食物的好滋味。

Allen 艾倫

I am extremely careful when there are kids and infants at a table. Hot plates, for example, are dangerous for these **daredevils**. They love to **grab**, to **bump into** others, and play around near and under the table. It makes me nervous just serving around them.

有兒童或嬰兒在場時，我會格外謹慎。比如說，熱騰騰的盤子對這些好奇寶寶來說就很危險。他們喜歡亂抓、彼此打鬧、並在桌邊和桌底下鑽來鑽去。在這些孩子附近送餐會讓我很緊張。

# 字彙和慣用語一覽表

| | | | |
|---|---|---|---|
| come along | 一起；偕同 | dine | v. 用餐 |
| unpredictable | adj. 無法預測的 | bomb | n. 炸彈 |
| ignite | v. 引爆 | least | adj. 最不…的 |
| duty | n. 義務 | convivial | adj. 歡樂的 |
| ambience | n. 氣氛 | basically | adv. 基本地 |
| praise | n. 讚美 | deserve | v. 應得 |
| bold | adj. 大膽的 | daredevil | n. 膽大的人 |
| grab | v. 拿取 | | |

**補充字彙**

| | | | |
|---|---|---|---|
| feast on sth | 吃…飽餐一頓 | unstable | adj. 不穩定的 |
| cordial | adj. 親切的 | in the air | 氣氛 |
| appraise | v. 評價；估價 | | |

# 好好用句型

本書一問三答中出現許多實用的句型或是短句，拿來練習最好不過了，現在也馬上試試看吧！看完之後，馬上就能輕鬆學會，不用背誦！

**句型一** ▶ **all for** 完全同意

**1** **Abby :** What about we take out four ingredients in the pantry, and see what we can make for dinner?

艾比：我們何不從食物儲藏櫃裡拿四樣材料，看看能做出什麼晚餐來？

**2** **Lydia :** I'm all for it. Let's do this!

莉迪亞：好耶，就這麼辦吧！

**句型二** ▶ **bump into** （肢體）撞上；碰巧遇見

**1** **Geoffrey :** I bumped into Katie yesterday. We ended up having dinner together.

傑弗瑞：我昨天碰巧遇見凱蒂，後來我們便共進晚餐。

**2** **June :** what a lovely coincidence!

珠兒：真是美麗的意外呀！

61

## 一問三答

When there is a birthday party reservation, it means a whole group of people and a lot of **noise**. Do you like to have birthday surprise parties in your restaurant?

當客人為了慶祝生日而訂位時，等於會有一大群人和噪音。你們喜歡客人在餐廳辦生日驚喜派對嗎？

Alina 艾琳娜

Who runs a restaurant and would not love to have a big group reservation? **True that** some people get too **excited** with their **celebration**, and they **disturb** other diners. But most of the time, people **behave** themselves, and they order a lot of food and drinks for the event. It's a good thing for us.

誰經營餐廳不想要有一大群人的預約呢？的確，有的人會在慶生的時

候太興奮，以至於影響到其他顧客。但大多時候，人們還是很守規矩的，而且他們會因為特別活動而點更多食物和飲料。這對我們來說是好事。

**Cathy 凱西**

It's a kitchen **nightmare** to have 20 tickets pouring in **all of a sudden**. Whenever we have a party reservation like that, it's always nerve-racking. I pray that they don't all order the same food, because if so we will have to keep them waiting for a little bit.

二十張點單一時之間湧入廚房，簡直是噩夢一場。當有人來餐廳辦派對之類的活動的時候，我總是如坐針氈。我總期望他們不會點同樣的料理，因為這樣我們就必須讓他們稍等一陣子。

**Allen 艾倫**

I love to have a birthday surprise party. It's like a special event in the daily **routine**! One time, I offered to sing the happy birthday song in German, and it was **_a big hit_**. I like to make people happy, **in short**. Plus, the **bonus** is usually good: a **generous** tip!

我喜歡有人來辦生日驚喜派對，這就像在平凡的日常中有特別活動一樣。有一次，我為壽星獻唱德文的生日快樂歌，結果大得迴響。總之，我喜歡讓別人開心，而且，附加價值也高，也就是會得到很多小費！

# 字彙和慣用語一覽表

| noise | n. 噪音 | excited | adj. 感到興奮的 |
|---|---|---|---|
| celebration | n. 慶祝 | disturb | v. 打擾 |
| behave | n. 行為 | nightmare | n. 夢魘 |
| all of a sudden | 突然之間 | routine | n. 例行公事 |
| in short | 總而言之 | bonus | n. 紅利 |
| generous | adj. 慷慨的 | | |

補充字彙

| hustling | adj. 忙亂的 | interrupt | v. 打岔；打擾 |
|---|---|---|---|
| out of blue | 突如其來地 | briefly | adv. 簡要地 |
| generously | adv. 慷慨地 | big-hearted | adj. 心胸寬大的 |
| agitated | adj. 激動的 | festive | adj. 歡樂的 |
| intense | adj. 激烈的 | | |

# 好好用句型

本書一問三答中出現許多實用的句型或是短句，拿來練習最好不過了，現在也馬上試試看吧！看完之後，馬上就能輕鬆學會，不用背誦！

**句型一 ▶ true that** 的確如此

**1 Lily :** My husband is so romantic. He gives me flowers all the time!

莉莉：我老公好浪漫，他常常送花給我。

**2 Peggy :** True that.

佩姬：的確很浪漫。

**句型二 ▶ a big hit** 造成大回響；事情很成功

**1 Wendy :** Did you go to Mr. Brown's speech last night?

溫蒂：妳昨晚有去聽布朗先生的演講嗎？

**2 Michelle :** Yeah, it was a big hit. I like his thinking.

蜜雪兒：有，那場演講很成功。我喜歡他的思考模式。

一問三答

 MP3 15

It happens that sometimes a customer has certain concerns about food, such as an allergy to seafood. How do you cope with this kind of special **condition individually**?

有時候客人會對特定食物有疑慮，比如說對海鮮過敏等，你們如何一一處理這些特殊狀況？

 *Alina* 艾琳娜

***Experience tells me that*** asking the customers **in advance** is more important than anything. Every food-related problem that happens in my place is a **shame**, even if we are not the **cause**. I always train my **employees** to ask our diners if they have any conditions like that.

按經驗來說，事先詢問客人比什麼都重要。在我的餐廳裡發生任何跟

食物有關的問題，不管是否肇因於我們，都是一件負面的事。我總是訓練員工主動詢問客人，看他們是否有任何這方面的問題。

*Cathy* 凱西

The question most commonly asked is if the food contains eggs. So many people are **allergic** to eggs, yet egg is a crucial **binding** ingredient for meatballs, burger **patties**, and pancakes ***to name a few***. So, we wrote it on the menu that if anyone needs an eggless meal, to please **inform** the server. This saves tons of work.

詢問度最高的問題是食物裡是否含蛋。太多人對蛋過敏，可是蛋卻是肉丸、漢堡排和鬆餅等料理中的重要連結原料。因此，我們就直接在菜單上標示，若有人需要無蛋料理，請告知服務生。這給我們省下不少功夫。

*Allen* 艾倫

I used to be **careless** when I first entered this industry. I didn't really care about the special orders of the customers, and I didn't know how our food was made, either. After a serious allergy **event** where a customer was taken to the hospital, I **dare** not be like that anymore.

我剛進餐飲業時相當粗枝大葉。我不關心客人的特殊需求，也不知道我們的餐點是怎麼做出來的。在一次嚴重的過敏事件，客人送醫之後，我就不敢再有這種態度了。

# 字彙和慣用語一覽表

| condition | n. 條件；狀況 | individually | adv. 個別地 |
|---|---|---|---|
| in advance | 事先 | shame | n. 羞恥 |
| cause | n. 原因 | employee | n. 員工 |
| allergic | adj. 過敏的 | binding | adj. 連接的 |
| patty | n. 肉餅 | inform | v. 告知 |
| careless | adj. 粗心的 | event | n. 事件 |
| dare | v. 敢 | | |

補充字彙

| illness | n. 疾病 | digestive | adj. 消化的 |
|---|---|---|---|
| discomfort | n. 不適 | choke | v. 梗塞 |
| disgrace | n. 不光彩的事 | infamous | adj. 惡名昭彰的 |
| unconcerned | adj. 漠不關心的 | | |

# 好好用句型

本書一問三答中出現許多實用的句型或是短句，拿來練習最好不過了，現在也馬上試試看吧！看完之後，馬上就能輕鬆學會，不用背誦！

**句型一 ▶ Experience tells me that** 根據經驗

1 **Debbie :** What outfit do you recommend for a first date?
黛比：妳推薦在第一次約會時穿什麼服裝？

2 **Olivia :** Experience tells me that pink dress always works out the best.
奧莉維亞：根據經驗，粉色洋裝最適合。

**句型二 ▶ to name a few** 僅列舉幾項；…等等

1 **Ken :** What kind of instrument can you play?
肯：你會彈什麼樂器？

2 **Paul :** Trumpet, piano, flute to name a few.
保羅：小號、鋼琴、長笛等等。

一問三答

It's quite common that a customer orders something, then changes it **later on**. Do you allow this to happen, and how do you *face it* if the food has already been prepared?

有時候客人點了某樣東西，之後卻更換所點的項目，這還滿常見的。你們允許這事發生嗎？如果餐點已開始製作，你們如何處置？

 *Alina* 艾琳娜

It's not **pleasant**, but I'll make the change. For me, the satisfaction of the diners is the first thing that I care about. Moreover, some dishes can be **heated up** again, such as pancakes and meatloaf, so it's not a **waste** every time.

這不太令人愉快，但我會做更動。對我來說，顧客滿意度是我最關心的事。其次，有些料理是可以再加熱的，例如鬆餅和肉派，所以不見得每次都會浪費食物。

Cathy 凱西

I **absolutely** hate it. Sometimes I really want to **yell** at those who *change their mind quicker than turning pages*. I'm just saying, though. When it happens like that, we have to follow the **command** from **above** us, which is to change the order as **directed**.

我很不喜歡這樣。有時候我真想對那些改變心意比翻書還快的人大吼，不過我也只是想想而已。當客人想改換餐點時，我們必須服從上頭的命令，也就是照客人要求的做更動。

Allen 艾倫

I'm not the one that makes the food, so I'm probably not that **annoyed**. However, I'm not **thrilled** to pass on this message to the kitchen. Because I am on the **polite** side, I'll tell the guest that I'll **negotiate** for them, but **sincerely** I don't like this to happen.

我不是煮飯的那個人，所以被惹惱的程度比較低。不過，要把這類訊息傳達給廚房，我也是不太樂意的。禮貌上，我告訴客人我會幫他們商量，但實際上我很不喜歡做這些事。

# 字彙和慣用語一覽表

| later on | 待會 | pleasant | adj. 令人愉悅的 |
|---|---|---|---|
| heat up | 加熱；升溫 | waste | n. 浪費 |
| absolutely | adv. 絕對地 | yell | v. 大吼；尖叫 |
| command | v. 指示；命令 | above | adj. 上面的 |
| direct | v. 指揮；指導 | annoyed | adj. 令人惱怒的 |
| thrilled | adj. 非常高興的 | polite | adj. 禮貌的 |
| negotiate | v. 協商；商談 | sincerely | adv. 真誠地 |

補充字彙

| agreeable | adj. 和藹的 | excess | adj. 多餘的 |
|---|---|---|---|
| surplus | n. 剩餘 | straightforward | adj. 直接了當的 |
| aggravated | adj. 惱人的 | gracious | adj. 親切、高尚的 |

# 好好用句型

本書一問三答中出現許多實用的句型或是短句，拿來練習最好不過了，現在也馬上試試看吧！看完之後，馬上就能輕鬆學會，不用背誦！

**句型一** ▶ **face sth.** 面對某事

**1** **Taylor :** Let's face it. You did say something silly on the Oscar Award.

泰勒斯：面對事實吧。妳的確在奧斯卡頒獎典禮上說了些不該說的話。

**2** **Laurence :** I think so. But I had to say it. I couldn't help.

勞倫斯：的確如此，但我一定得那樣說，我別無選擇。

**句型二** ▶ **change sb's mind quicker than turning pages** 形容人改變心意之快速

**1** **Jennifer :** I decide not to go to the prom with you.

珍妮佛：我決定不跟你去畢業舞會了。

**2** **Jeff :** Come on! How could you change your mind quicker than turning pages?

傑夫：別這樣，妳怎麼可以翻臉比翻書還快？

# 4.3 Running out of food
# 食材用完了

 **Q&A 一問三答**

 MP3 17

During a busy service, if one or multiple ingredients run out, will you **cross out** certain items on the menu? If you don't, how do you **improvise**?

在尖峰時段，如果一兩樣食材用罄，你們會停止供應菜單上的項目嗎？若是不會，你們如何應變？

 Alina 艾琳娜

It depends on which ingredient runs out. If rice is out, making a new batch takes about 25 minutes. That's not **a big deal**. But if **pulled pork** runs out, let's just **call it a day** on that item. Normally, I do my best to meet every need of our guests, but if I can't, then that's that.

要看是什麼食材用罄，如果米飯沒了，煮一鍋大約要二十五分鐘，這

74

不成問題。但要是手撕豬肉售完，就只能這麼辦了。通常我盡可能地去滿足顧客的要求，但如果我做不到的話，也就只能如此了。

Quite **frequently**, what we run out of are the side dishes. Bok choy, baby spinach, coleslaw, etc. We still need them to complete our main course, so I'm trained to move very fast. Take coleslaw for example, I'll use a cheese grater to quickly **shave up** a cabbage and *whip it up*.

很常發生配菜不足的情況，例如青江菜、幼菠菜葉或涼拌捲心菜等。我們還是需要這些配菜來完成整道主菜，因此我的動作被訓練得越來越快。舉涼拌捲心菜為例，我會用起司刨刀很快地削完一顆高麗菜，然後做出涼拌捲心菜來。

I get really nervous when something is out and the plates are **piling up**. One time, I needed to **garnish** six plates of **ravioli** with freshly **chopped** parsley, but there's not even a **shred** of it available. I just **freaked out**. Now I check these kinds of garnishes every time before service.

如果很多菜等著要出，卻有食材用完，我會變得很緊張。有次我必須用巴西里葉裝飾六盤義大利餃，但連一株巴西里葉都沒有。我不知所措。現在，每次上工前我都會看看這些裝飾是否足夠。

**字彙和慣用語一覽表**

| cross out | 劃掉；打叉 | improvise | v. 即興創作 |
|---|---|---|---|
| a big deal | 大事；嚴重的事 | pulled pork | 手撕豬肉 |
| frequently | adv. 經常地 | shave up | 削（蔬菜） |
| pile up | 堆成一疊 | garnish | v. 裝飾 |
| ravioli | n. 義大利餃 | chop | v. 切 |
| shred | n. 碎片；細條 | freak out | 嚇壞；慌了手腳 |

補充字彙

| make a fuss | 小題大作 | regularly | adv. 經常地 |
|---|---|---|---|
| décor | n. 裝飾 | poach | v. 水煮；油煮 |
| broil | v. 上火燒烤 | slice | v. 切成細片 |
| stew | v. 燉煮 | blanch | v. 清燙 |

# 好好用句型

本書一問三答中出現許多實用的句型或是短句，拿來練習最好不過了，現在也馬上試試看吧！看完之後，馬上就能輕鬆學會，不用背誦！

**句型一 ▶ call it a day** 就此結束

1 **Justin :** Do you think we should make more cheesecake and croissants?
賈斯汀：妳覺得我們要再多做起司蛋糕和可頌嗎？

2 **Jane :** No, let's just call it a day.
珍：不，今天就到此為止吧。

**句型二 ▶ whip sth. up / whip up sth.** 很快地變出某物／完成某事

1 **David :** How could you make skirt steak sandwich and brownie in just an hour?
大衛：妳是怎麼在一小時內做出橫膈牛三明治和布朗尼的？

2 **Nancy :** Well, I just whip them up!
南茜：做一做就出來了呀。

# 4.4 Breaking Tableware
# 打破餐具

Tableware being broken must be *nothing new* for a restaurant. The **accidents** around the table **challenge** one's ability to deal with **emergencies**. What's your policy and **procedure** for this kind of situation?

打破餐具對餐廳來說是家常便飯。這些發生在客人桌邊的意外，挑戰著一個人面對緊急事故的應變能力。你們對這種情況的策略和程序是什麼呢？

Alina 艾琳娜

First of all, it makes a difference whether our employees or the customers broke the tableware. If our servers broke it, depending on the **frequency** and the **level** of the loss, I have to decide one's **liability**. It's **cruel**, I know, but it's **logical**. I want our guests to feel at home, not to be **frightened**.

首先，要看是員工打破東西，還是顧客，這有所不同。如果是服務生打破的，依照頻繁度和損失程度，我必須決定其去留。的確殘酷，但很合邏輯。我希望我們的客人都賓至如歸，而不是膽戰心驚。

Cathy 凱西

Count it as bad luck if anything breaks on the table that you're responsible for. Sometimes, even with all your **concentration**, the plates will **slip off** your hand. **In terms of** our customers, it is best to **reseat** them at another table, especially when there is a wet **tablecloth** or broken glasses.

如果你負責的桌次發生東西摔破的事件，就當作是運氣不好吧。有時候就算你已全神貫注，盤子還是會從手中滑出去。至於客人的處置，最好讓他們換位子，尤其是在桌巾濕掉或有碎玻璃的情況下。

Allen 艾倫

Replacing broken glasses isn't so bad; what gives me a big headache is cleaning up the **spilled** liquid, sometimes hot soup. Young kids will definitely need plastic tableware. Trust me, it *saves you a lot of headaches*. As for myself, I try not to carry too many dirty plates at once. Less chance to have anything fall.

換上新的玻璃杯不是難事，讓我頭大的是清理潑出來的液體或熱湯。小孩子絕對需要塑膠餐具，相信我，這會省下很多麻煩。至於我本身，我不會一次拿太多髒碟子，這會減少東西掉落的機會。

# 字彙和慣用語一覽表

| | | | |
|---|---|---|---|
| accident | n. 意外 | challenge | v. 挑戰 |
| emergency | n. 緊急事件 | procedure | n. 程序 |
| frequency | n. 頻繁度 | level | n. 等級；程度 |
| liability | n. 責任、義務 | cruel | adj. 殘酷的 |
| logical | adj. 有邏輯的 | frighten | v. 使害怕 |
| concentration | n. 集中注意 | slip off | 飛出；滑走 |
| in terms of | 關於… | reseat | v. 使再次就坐 |
| tablecloth | n. 桌巾 | spill | v. 潑灑 |

補充字彙

| | | | |
|---|---|---|---|
| incident | n. 偶發事件 | regularity | n. 規律性 |
| legality | adj. 合法性 | brutal | adj. 野蠻的 |
| distraction | n. 干擾 | awareness | n. 注意；覺察 |

# 好好用句型

本書一問三答中出現許多實用的句型或是短句，拿來練習最好不過了，現在也馬上試試看吧！看完之後，馬上就能輕鬆學會，不用背誦！

句型一 ▶ **nothing new** 不是新鮮事／常有的事

1 **Howard :** Jimmy slipped the class today.
霍華：米吉今天翹課了。

2 **Chuck :** That's nothing new. He does that all the time.
恰克：這不是什麼新鮮事，他常常這樣。

句型二 ▶ **save sb. the headache** 幫某人省下麻煩

1 **Roy :** What if I don't give you my soul? What if I say no?
羅伊：如果不給你我的靈魂呢？如果我說不的話呢？

2 **Devil :** Come on, just save me the headache.
惡魔：別這樣，讓我省省麻煩吧。

## Q&A 一問三答

Being a server, it must happen a lot that the **delicacy** arrives at the table, yet you **discover** that it has **landed** in the wrong **territory**. What do you do to **resolve** the **embarrassing scene**?

身為一個服務生，一定發生過美食拿到桌邊，才發現自己送錯桌的糗事。你們如何化解這樣尷尬的場面？

*Alina* 艾琳娜

I don't serve the food a lot, so when I do, I make sure that this situation doesn't take place. If I were the diner, I would see this restaurant as an **unorganized**, **disastrous** place if the food came to the wrong table. This is a serious matter and I want my employees to be *on the same page*.

我不常送餐，所以只要我有送，我便會確保這個情況不會發生。如果

我是顧客，我會覺得一間餐點送錯桌的店家不嚴謹、沒有員工訓練。這是個嚴重的問題，而我要我的員工都了解這件事的重要性。

Cathy 凱西

I wanted to say that just an **apology _won't hurt_**. However, it's not that simple. Even if the customers don't mind, I will get **alerted** and double check the table number the next time. You never know who you are serving the food to, and a **displeased** food **critic** can really hurt the business.

我本想告訴你道歉即可，事情不嚴重。然而，其實沒有這麼簡單。就算客人不在意，我也會緊張起來，並在下次送餐時重複確認桌號。你永遠不知道你送餐的對象是誰，而一則負面美食評論可是能重創我們的生意呢。

Allen 艾倫

The best solution is to smile. Smiling and **making** some **fun of** yourself can definitely help. Many times, it's not the customers that get mad; actually, most of them are pretty understanding. It's my **employers**. For them, this is a **negative** situation and I've been **scolded** many times.

最好的解決方法就是笑。微笑並調侃自己絕對有用。很多時候，不是顧客生氣，其實，大部分的顧客都很善解人意。是老闆會生氣。對他們來説，這是個扣分的舉動，我已經被罵過很多次了。

# 字彙和慣用語一覽表

| | | | |
|---|---|---|---|
| delicacy | n. 美饌 | discover | v. 發現 |
| land | v. 降落 | territory | n. 領土 |
| resolve | v. 解決 | embarrassing | adj. 令人尷尬的 |
| scene | n. 場面 | unorganized | adj. 無組織的 |
| disastrous | adj. 災難的 | apology | n. 道歉 |
| alerted | adj. 受警告的 | displeased | adj. 不開心的 |
| critic | n. 評論；評論家 | make fun of | 取笑 |
| employer | n. 雇主 | negative | adj. 負面的 |
| scold | v. 責罵 | | |

補充字彙

| | | | |
|---|---|---|---|
| subtlety | n. 纖細；微妙 | patron | n. 老主顧 |
| make a scene | 使人難堪 | muddle | v. 隨便應付 |

好好用句型

本書一問三答中出現許多實用的句型或是短句，拿來練習最好不過了，現在也馬上試試看吧！看完之後，馬上就能輕鬆學會，不用背誦！

句型一 ▶ **on the same page** 有共識

1 **Claire :** I want to make sure that everyone is on the same page and no errors occur.
克萊兒：我想確定每個人都有共識了，才不會造成失誤。

2 **Brandy :** Sure. You can count on us.
布蘭迪：當然，妳就相信我們吧。

句型二 ▶ **sth. won't hurt** 做（某事）不會怎麼樣；不會少一塊肉

1 **Bob :** I have no interest in going to the park. I just want to be a couch potato.
鮑伯：我一點也不想去公園，我只想吃零食看電視。

2 **Lisa :** A little exercise won't hurt!
莉莎：做點運動又不會怎麼樣。

# 5.1 Shortage on the food
# 食材短缺

There is an **unpredictability** of orders. If the food **runs out**, will you **cancel** the order? For instance, everybody orders mashed potatoes, yet daily amount is **fixed**. How would you **respond** to customers who order later, but **are unable to** get the mashed potatoes?

客人點單總是不確定，如果食材不幸售罄，你們會取消點單嗎？譬如：每個人都點馬鈴薯泥，但每日製作的量是固定的，對後來點餐卻無法取得馬鈴薯泥的客人，你們如何應對？

 *Alina* 艾琳娜

There's no way that we're gonna tell and return the **tickets**. Even though we are running out of food, we don't **turn** the customers **down**. Since we won't cancel the order, making a new **batch** is *the way to go*. This is our highest **policy**.

絕不可以拒絕客人的點餐。就算食材真的售罄，我們也不會拒絕客人。既然我們不會取消點單，就必須趕快做新的一份，這是我們的最高原則。

Cathy 凱西

If we just blind them and tell them to wait for an **uncertain** amount of time, not only are they not promised to get the food, but also they will have a poor experience **dining** in our restaurant. I **figure that** telling them we are out of food and suggesting other **options** may be *the wiser thing to do*.

如果我們呼攏客人，告訴他們必須等，但不告訴他們要等多久，這不僅對客人沒保障，說不定還會讓他們對我們餐廳的印象變差。我發現最好的方法是誠實告知食材售完，並建議客人點別道菜。

Allen 艾倫

If the **item** that I want is sold out, I'd like to know the truth. If so, I can decide whether I should stay and **pick up** another item on the menu, or just go somewhere else **instead**. Letting customers have the **right** to choose is better than **telling lies**.

如果我點的菜賣光，我想知道實情，這樣才能決定是要留下來點別道菜，還是要去其他餐廳。讓客人有選擇權會比說謊好。

# 字彙和慣用語一覽表

| | | | |
|---|---|---|---|
| shortage | n. 短缺 | unpredictability | n. 不可預測性 |
| run out | 用完 | cancel | v. 取消 |
| fixed | adj. 固定的 | respond | v. 反應 |
| be unable to | 無法做… | ticket | n. 點單 |
| turn down | 拒絕 | batch | n. 批 |
| policy | n. 方針;政策 | uncertain | adj. 不確定的 |
| dine | v. 用餐 | figure that… | 發現;覺得 |
| option | n. 選項 | item | n. 物件 |
| pick up | 選擇 | instead | 而不是… |
| right | n. 權力 | tell lies | 說謊 |

**好好用句型**

本書一問三答中出現許多實用的句型或是短句，拿來練習最好不過了，現在也馬上試試看吧！看完之後，馬上就能輕鬆學會，不用背誦！

句型一 ▶ **the way to go** 處理方法就是如此

**1** **Jack :** What should I do to bring my girlfriend back to me?

傑克：我該怎麼做才能挽回女友的心？

**2** **John :** Being honest is the way to go.

約翰：誠實以對是最好的方法。

句型二 ▶ **the wiser thing to do** 明智之舉

**1** **Rosie :** It's raining outside. Do you think I should still repair my car in the yard?

蘿絲：外面在下雨耶，你覺得我還要不要到院子裡修車呢？

**2** **Ken :** Jest leave it. Keep yourself warm is a wiser thing to do.

肯：不要吧，保暖比較重要。

**一問三答**

MP3
21

> In the kitchen, there's this **craziness** that makes a wrong ticket a common mistake. How to **fix** this mistake other than eat the food yourself?
>
> 在廚房裡，混亂的狀況常導致餐點製作錯誤。除了自己吃掉這份餐之外，還有什麼方法能解決這個狀況呢？

*Alina* 艾琳娜

There is no way that a wrong order will take place under my **supervision**. When I'm *in charge*, I won't let those kinds of mistakes **pass through**. Every ticket needs to be cared for, even in the busiest hour. It's all about experience, I will say.

做錯餐點這事絕不會在我眼皮底下發生。當我在廚房坐鎮時，我不會讓這種錯誤過關。每張點單都必須留意，就算在最忙的時候也一樣。

這跟經驗有關。

Cathy 凱西

Sometimes ***it's a matter of*** whether you get mad at yourself, or try to **convince** the customer. If it's not a serious error, such as having made **squid** instead of shrimp, I may just tell them that the squid is fresher and see if they want squid instead.

有時候就只是看你要對自己生氣，還是要去説服客人。如果錯誤不嚴重，例如把蝦子做成墨魚，我可能會告訴客人墨魚比較新鮮，看他們要不要換點墨魚。

Allen 艾倫

I think I'll just blame myself and feel **ashamed**. Because I'm the **least** experienced, and I do **mishear** the customers sometimes. Alina has **punished** me by **taking up** the loss in my pay, and I think that's **understandable**. I just have to try harder so that this won't happen too often.

我想我會自責並對自己生氣吧，因為我是最菜的一個，而且我的確曾誤聽客人的點餐。艾琳娜已經用扣薪的方式處罰過我了，我覺得也是合情理。我必須更努力，減少這種錯誤的發生。

# 字彙和慣用語一覽表

| craziness | n. 瘋狂 | fix | v. 修理；修復 |
|---|---|---|---|
| supervision | n. 監督 | pass through | 通過；過關 |
| convince | v. 說服 | squid | n. 墨魚；花枝 |
| ashamed | adj. 羞愧地 | least | adj. 最不⋯的 |
| mishear | v. 誤聽 | punish | v. 懲罰 |
| take up | 負責 | understandable | adj. 可理解的 |
| 補充字彙 | | | |
| insanity | n. 狂亂 | management | n. 管理 |
| persuade | v. 勸說 | talk sb. into | 說服某人做某事 |
| misunderstand | v. 誤會；誤解 | rebuke | v. 訓斥；責罵 |
| reasonable | adj. 合理的 | logical | adj. 有邏輯的 |

# 好好用句型

本書一問三答中出現許多實用的句型或是短句，拿來練習最好不過了，現在也馬上試試看吧！看完之後，馬上就能輕鬆學會，不用背誦！

句型一 ▶ **in charge** （人）決定、有權利

1 **Ina :** What do you say we go out for dinner tonight?
伊娜：今晚出外用餐怎麼樣？

2 **Remi :** You're in charge.
瑞米：都聽妳的。

句型二 ▶ **it's a matter of** 是⋯的問題

1 **Greg :** That murderer needs to be put under justice!
桂格：那個兇手必須被繩之以法！

2 **Kimberley :** He can't get away forever. It's just a matter of time.
金柏莉：他不可能永遠逍遙法外，只是時間的問題而已。

# 5.3 Too Slow 出餐過慢

When there are too many tickets, **it seems that** no matter how fast you move, the tickets are always piled up there. When the **ability** of the kitchen to **keep up** is **limited** and complaints of customers are coming, how to deal with them and find yourself **balance** in the kitchen?

客人眾多時，無論你動作多快，點單似乎永遠消化不完。當你的動作已經到了極限，而客人卻還是在抱怨時，要如何處理客訴，並在廚房找到平衡點呢？

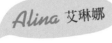
Alina 艾琳娜

In the food industry, this is **inevitable**. It's better to be busy than to be **bored**, isn't it? ***That being said***, I do get **grumpy** when the tickets are piled up. It's **stressful**. I need to **race** with the clock. My

**solution** is to **gulp down** a shot of **expresso**.

在餐飲業裡，這是無法避免的狀況。忙碌總比沒客人好，對吧？雖說如此，點單堆積如山時，我的確會顯得暴躁，因為壓力很大。我必須跟時間賽跑，而紓解方案是大口吞下義式濃縮咖啡。

*Cathy* 凱西

Try not to make any mistakes, that's the first priority. We are a popular restaurant, so we are **crowded** at lunch time. There is no time to fix somebody's steak or do an eggs benedict **over again**. I always feel nervous, because *the devil is in the details*.

試著別犯錯，這是第一要務。我們餐廳很熱門，午餐時間總是相當忙碌，而我不會有時間去處理客人的牛排問題，或重作一份班尼迪克蛋。我總是戰戰兢兢，因為魔鬼藏在細節裡。

*Allen* 艾倫

It's nerve-racking. My duty is to bring orders to the kitchen, and if the customers complain about the **delay** on their dishes, yet the kitchen is so **backed up**, there's nothing I can do. I can only try my best to **console** the customers before their food arrives.

這很令人緊張。我的工作是將點單送進廚房，如果客人抱怨送餐慢，廚房卻已經忙得暈頭轉向時，我實在也不能做什麼。我盡量在餐點送達前多安撫客人就是了。

# 字彙和慣用語一覽表

| it seems that | 似乎 | ability | n. 能力 |
| --- | --- | --- | --- |
| keep up | 跟上 | limited | adj. 受限制的 |
| balance | n. 平衡 | inevitable | adj. 無法避免的 |
| bored | adj. 感到無聊的 | grumpy | adj. 脾氣差的 |
| stressful | adj. 有壓力的 | race | v. 競賽；賽跑 |
| solution | n. 解決方案 | gulp down | 牛飲；大口吞 |
| expresso | n. 義式濃縮咖啡 | crowded | adj. 擁擠的 |
| over again | 再一次 | delay | n. 拖遲 |
| backed up | 忙碌的 | console | v. 安撫 |

補充字彙

| full house | 客滿狀態 | compete | v. 比賽 |
| --- | --- | --- | --- |

# 好好用句型

本書一問三答中出現許多實用的句型或是短句，拿來練習最好不過了，現在也馬上試試看吧！看完之後，馬上就能輕鬆學會，不用背誦！

**句型一 ▶ That being said** 雖說如此

**1** **Alex :** Your fish is sinfully overcooked. That being said, the sauce is delicious.
艾莉克絲：你的魚嚴重煮過頭，不過，醬汁倒是非常美味。

**2** **Julien :** Thank you.
朱利安：謝謝。

**句型二 ▶ the devil is in the details** 注意細節

**1** **Aaron :** Grilling fish is all about the crispy skin. Soggy skin is such a shame.
艾倫：烤魚時最重要的就是酥脆的外皮，若魚皮軟爛就可惜了。

**2** **Amanda :** The devil is in the details, isn't it?
艾曼達：魔鬼藏在細節裡，對吧？

# 5.4 Cut Oneself
# 切到自己

Have you ever cut yourself in the kitchen? It's a problem that needs to be dealt with seriously. You can't *go easy with* contamination.

你們是否曾在廚房裡切到自己過呢？這是必須慎重以待的問題，食物污染是不能被輕忽的。

Alina 艾琳娜

I *can't agree with you more*. One of the most fatal problems in the kitchen is to prepare the food with unclean hands. Hairs, bleeding, and nail polish are strictly prohibited in the kitchen. We don't want to serve food that contains these items, do we? Healthy food is our promise to the customers.

我非常同意。廚房裡最致命的問題之一，就是用不乾淨的手料理食材。頭髮、血液、指甲油在廚房裡都是嚴格禁止的。我們不希望我們

提供的食物裡混雜這些東西，對吧？健康的料理是我們對顧客的承諾。

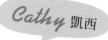

Never, ever use **bare** hands to touch the ingredients when there's a **wound**. Whether it's a deep **cut** or not, **bleeding** or not, there are **invisible germs invading** and **polluting** everything that it contacts. Using a Band-Aid and gloves won't slow you down. After all, I don't want to get this place **shut down** and lose my job.

手上有傷口的話，千萬不可以赤手調理食物。不論傷口大或小、是否流血，無形的細菌都會沾染並汙染所有觸摸到的東西。使用OK繃不會妨礙工作的，畢竟我可不想害這裡關門大吉，我自己也失業。

It's literally **a matter of life or death**. Food contamination is so crucial yet so easy to be neglected. Working in this industry is all about one's heart. We want to **provide** natural, hearty meals, not bacteria **infested** food that gets people sick. Alina and Cathy **insist** on this point very much. I **look up to** them.

這是名副其實的生死攸關之事。食品汙染非同小可，但卻容易受到忽視。在這個產業工作，最重要的就是個人的良心。我們想提供的是自然、暖心的美食，而非受到細菌汙染、害人生病的食物。艾琳娜和凱西非常堅持這點，我也很尊敬她們。

# 字彙和慣用語一覽表

| | | | |
|---|---|---|---|
| contamination | n. 汙染 | fatal | adj. 致命的 |
| unclean | adj. 不潔的 | nail polish | n. 指甲油 |
| strictly | adv. 嚴格地 | prohibit | v. 禁止；阻止 |
| bare | adj. 赤裸的；空的 | wound | n. 傷口 |
| cut | n. 傷口 | bleed | v. 流血 |
| invisible | adj. 隱形的 | germ | n. 細菌 |
| invade | v. 入侵 | pollute | v. 汙染 |
| shut down | 關店；封鎖 | a matter of life or death | 生死攸關之事 |
| provide | v. 供應 | infest | v. 充斥；寄生 |
| insist | v. 堅持 | look up to | 景仰；尊敬 |
| 補充字彙 | | | |
| infection | n.（病毒）感染 | claim | v. 主張；宣稱 |

## 好好用句型

本書一問三答中出現許多實用的句型或是短句，拿來練習最好不過了，現在也馬上試試看吧！看完之後，馬上就能輕鬆學會，不用背誦！

**句型一** ▶ **go easy with** 對…等閒視之

**1 Karen :** Leaving candles on while we are sleeping is romantic!

凱倫：睡覺時點著蠟燭很浪漫呢！

**2 Ivan :** Don't ever go easy with fire. It's dangerous. You can burn the whole place down!

伊凡：火焰不能等閒視之，這很危險，可能會把整棟房子給燒了！

**句型二** ▶ **can't agree with sb. more** 非常同意某人

**1 Titan :** It's so refreshing to have mango shaved ice in a summer day.

泰坦：炎炎夏日有芒果冰吃真是太消暑了。

**2 Julia :** I can't agree with you more.

茱莉亞：說得太對了。

一問三答

If you walk into the kitchen, and **figure out** that the necessary **goods** are not prepared, what will you do to solve the problem?

如果你們走進廚房,發現有必要食材沒有準備好,你們會怎麼解決問題呢?

Alina 艾琳娜

First of all, if it's somebody's **laziness** that **caused** the problem, they are gonna be in big trouble! I always go to the kitchen three or four hours before service **out of fear** that this **situation** will **take place**. If it does, I will prepare the ingredients **ASAP**.

第一,如果這是某個傢伙的懶散導致的,他們就有大麻煩了。我常常提早三、四小時進廚房,就是怕有這種情況發生。如果真的發生了,

我會盡快準備食材。

Cathy 凱西

It will be **a pain in the ass** but you won't die. I mean, the loss is not on me if something's not ready to be sold today. Still, I have to solve the problem, and the secret is to move really fast.

這真的很麻煩，但還不至於要我的命。我是說，如果有東西沒準備好，當天不能賣，損失也不是算在我頭上。不過，我還是得解決問題，而秘訣是動作快！

Allen 艾倫

I'll take a deep **breath** and try to figure out a way to prepare the **necessities** as quickly as possible. For instance, if the meat is still frozen, I'll **thaw** it in the microwave. But if the stock is not enough, I **suppose** that I will have to be prepared to **start cooking**.

深呼吸，然後試著想出快速準備必要食材的方法。例如，如果肉還是冷凍的，我會丟到微波爐裡解凍。但如果高湯煮不夠，我要重新準備才能開始煮。

# 字彙和慣用語一覽表

| | | | |
|---|---|---|---|
| figure out | 找出 | goods | n. 貨物；商品 |
| laziness | n. 懶散 | cause | v. 造成 |
| situation | n. 狀況 | take place | 發生 |
| ASAP | 立刻 | breath | n. 呼吸 |
| necessities | n. 必需品 | thaw | v. 解凍 |
| suppose | v. 認為 | be cooked | 被罵；完蛋了 |
| 補充字彙 | | | |
| procrastinator | n. 很會拖延的人 | breathe | v. 呼吸 |
| provision | n. 預防措施 | defrost | v. 解凍；除霜 |
| overlook | v. 忽略 | recall | v. 想起 |
| assume | v. 設想；假定 | reckon | v. 估計；推算 |

# 好好用句型

本書一問三答中出現許多實用的句型或是短句,拿來練習最好不過了,現在也馬上試試看吧!看完之後,馬上就能輕鬆學會,不用背誦!

**句型一 ▶ out of fear** 出於恐懼

1 **Suzanne :** My son goes to math class out of fear that he will fall behind in his class.

蘇珊:我兒子因為怕課程進度跟不上,而去上數學加強班。

2 **Ray :** He is a hard-working boy.

蕾:他真是個認真向上的孩子。

**句型二 ▶ a pain in the ass** 麻煩事

1 **Romano :** The new guy calls in sick again.

羅馬諾:新來的員工又打來請假了。

2 **Cecilia :** He is such a pain in the ass!

西利雅:他真是麻煩。

105

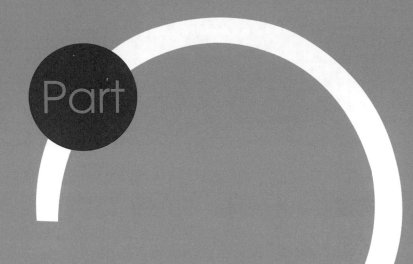

Part

# 餐飲搶分篇

2

## 學習進度表

看完後別忘了打勾喔！

# Reception
# 招呼與帶位

*Allen* / 店員

*Customer* / 客人

 **情境對話**

**Allen :** Good evening! How are you?

艾倫：晚上好，您們好嗎？

**Customer 1 :** Great! We are excited about tonight. We love this place.

客人一：很好，我們很興奮，因為我們都很喜歡這間餐廳。

**Allen :** Awesome! How many people are with you?

艾倫：太棒了。您們共幾位？

**Customer 1 :** We have four people.

客人一：我們有四個人。

**Allen :** Right this way, please.

艾倫：請跟我來。

**Customer 1 :** Oh, can we not sit near the air conditioner? It's kind of **chilly**.

客人一：噢，我們可以不要坐在空調附近嗎？有點冷。

**Allen :** No problem. **My apology**, ma'am. I'm your server for tonight. My name is Allen. You may take a look at the menu, and I'll come back later for your drinks.

艾倫：沒問題，很抱歉，女士。我是您們今晚的服務生，我叫做艾倫。請您們先看看菜單，我待會兒會來幫您們點飲料。

**Customers :** Thank you.

客人們：謝謝。

**Allen :** What do you need to drink?

艾倫：您們想喝些什麼？

**Customer 2 :** I'll have an **electric** mojito.

客人二：我要電擊薄荷調酒。

**Allen :** Of course. May I see your ID, sir?

艾倫：沒問題。先生，我可以看看您的身分證嗎？

**Customer 2 :** There you go.

客人二：在這兒。

**Allen :** Thank you. I'll be right back.

艾倫：謝謝您，我待會就回來。

# 哪裡有問題

服務生帶位時，需要確知一組來客數、客人的組成及座位需求。文中的客人不想坐在空調附近，這有可能是客人中有年長者的關係。帶位時，服務生應盡可能的觀察客人的組成，並將其安置在合適的位置，例如帶小孩的家長應坐在較寬敞的位子，讓孩子有空間嬉鬧、情侶則適合安排在角落的雙人座位等。

另外，需注意歐美的用餐習慣是在就座後立刻點飲料。

# 餐飲補充包

The restaurant culture in the West is quite different from the one in Asia. Usually, the drink order is taken right after the guests **are seated**. If new faces come to the restaurant, they may have to **browse** through the menu **in a rush**. In the breakfast-brunch **kind of** diner, the orders are likely to be cokes, seven-ups or coffee. In the **formal** dining restaurant, **on the other hand**, **alcoholic beverages** are quite **frequent**.

If the restaurant **features** special **cocktails** or **craft** beers, the server may introduce them to the diners simultaneously. This can not only leave a good impression for the restaurant, but also **boost** profits, since alcohol is rather **costly** comparing to other items.

Something to be **cautious** about is the legal drinking age. According to the U.S. law, only people over 21 can have alcohol. Hence, the server must check the customer's ID to **ensure** one's **legality**.

# 中譯

歐美的餐館文化與亞洲的習慣大不相同，常在就座後立刻點飲料，若是客人第一次到這間餐廳，可能會來不及看菜單。若在早午餐類的餐館，客人常點可樂、七喜等氣泡飲品或咖啡；若是晚餐時段的正式餐館，客人則常點酒精飲品。

若是該店有特色風味雞尾酒或精釀啤酒，可在客人點飲料時主動介紹，除了讓來客對該店留下印象外，也能促進消費，畢竟酒精飲品的費用都是偏高的。

需要留意的是各國法定飲酒年齡，美國喝酒的合法年齡是二十一歲，服務生必須對照客人證件，確定客人是合法飲酒年齡，否則將有觸法危險。

# 字彙和慣用語一覽表

| | | | |
|---|---|---|---|
| chilly | adj. 寒冷的 | my apology | 我的不對、抱歉 |
| electric | adj. 電氣的 | be seated | =sit down |
| browse | v. 瀏覽 | in a rush | 匆忙的 |
| kind of | …之類的 | formal | adj. 正式的 |
| on the other hand | 另一面來說 | alcoholic | adj. 酒精的 |
| beverage | n. 飲料 | frequent | adj. 頻繁的 |
| feature | v. 以…為特色 | cocktail | n. 雞尾酒 |
| craft | n. 手藝 | boost | v. 促進 |
| costly | adj. 昂貴的 | cautious | adj. 謹慎的 |
| ensure | v. 確保 | legality | n. 合法性 |

Part
2
餐飲搶分篇

Unit
01

Dining Service 點餐服務及餐間服務

# Unit 1.2 Menu Introduction 介紹餐點

 Allen / 店員

 Customer / 客人

 情境對話  MP3 26

**Customer 1 :** I'm pretty curious about your special Italian menu. Can you introduce some dishes for us?

客人一：我對你們的義大利特別菜單感到很好奇，可以請你幫我們介紹一些餐點嗎？

**Allen :** Of course. Our **signature dish** is macaroni and cheese. It's made with American cheddar sauce and chicken **cubes**, topped with a thin layer of crushed Ritz crackers and Italian spiced bread crumbs. We also put **caramelized** onion

艾倫：當然可以。我們的招牌菜是焗烤通心粉。由美國切達起司醬和雞肉塊組成，上面是一層薄薄的莉茲餅乾屑和義大利香料麵包粉。我們也在醬汁裡加入焦糖洋蔥和炒過的大蒜。

and sautéed garlic in the sauce.

**Customer 1 :** Sounds good.

**Allen :** It's very delicious. We also have great pasta dishes, such as shrimp scampi, seafood sauté, and chicken cacciatore. We make our marinara sauce with fresh tomatoes, right from the farmer's market in the neighborhood.

**Customer 2 :** That's awesome. Supporting the locals.

**Allen :** Yes, we **aim to** have the freshest ingredients so that our customers can enjoy the food without any concerns.

客人一：聽起來不錯。

艾倫：非常好吃。我們的義大利麵也很不錯，例如白酒炒明蝦、海鮮義大利麵和獵人燉雞。我們使用社區裡的農夫市集買來的新鮮番茄做紅醬。

客人二：真棒，支持在地。

艾倫：是的，我們旨在使用最新鮮的材料，讓客人們可以無後顧之憂地享用料理。

# 哪裡有問題

當客人要求介紹菜單時，服務生將瞬間成為當天點餐的決定性關鍵。有些餐廳基於業績考量，會要求員工推薦該店較昂貴的菜餚，然而員工是否能真誠的推薦，其實顧客都是能察覺出來的。文中艾倫是以店中較為特殊的餐點為推薦的主力，例如加入麗姿餅乾屑的焗烤通心粉等，力求讓客人留下「本店與眾不同」的印象。

## 餐飲補充包

Menu introduction is a **critical** mission of a server. Besides the fact that when the table has higher **expenses**, the server will get more tips. Using a few minutes to impress the customers is the **privilege** of the responsible server.

Being the mission **executor**, it is necessary for one to taste every single dish that's on the menu. If possible, one should **savor** every dish and decide on **phrases** to use while introducing the menu. Depending on how the server **describes** the menu, the choices of the diners may change **dramatically**.

One may **highlight** on two parts in the introduction: the taste and the **cookery**. **Assume that** a dish is **stunningly luscious**, and it's the best-seller, it should be recommended first. Or, if the restaurant **interprets** a classic dish in a modern way, it is worth recommendation, too.

# 中譯

介紹餐點對服務生來說是相當重要的任務，除了該桌消費較高時，服務生能獲得的小費也較多之外，如何利用桌邊的一、兩分鐘加深顧客對餐廳的印象，也是只有負責該桌的服務生才有的特權。

身為此任務的執行者，自己能確實品嘗過每道菜單上的菜餚是不可或缺的。若是可能的話，必須盡可能的品嘗每道菜，並事先練習介紹菜單的順序及用詞。根據服務生的描述，將大大改變顧客的選擇。

介紹餐點可以著重在兩方面：味道及烹調方式。若是某道菜驚為天人的美味，銷量極佳，可以率先推薦；抑或是某道菜將經典料理以創新的手法烹調，也很值得推薦。

# 字彙和慣用語一覽表

| | | | |
|---|---|---|---|
| signature dish | 拿手菜 | cube | n. 塊狀 |
| caramelize | v. 使焦糖化 | aim to | 旨在 |
| tons of work | 很費工 | critical | adj. 要緊的 |
| expense | n. 花費 | privilege | n. 特權 |
| executor | n. 執行者 | savor | v. 品味 |
| phrase | n. 用詞 | describe | v. 描述 |
| dramatically | adv. 顯著地 | highlight | v. 著重於 |
| cookery | n. 烹調法 | assume that | 試想… |
| stunningly | adv. 令人驚訝地 | luscious | adj. 甜美、豐盛的 |
| interpret | v. 詮釋 | | |

# Unit 1.3 Order 點餐

 *Allen* / 店員　　 *Customer* / 客人

 **情境對話**

**Allen :** You guys ready? Can I take the order? Or do you need another second?

艾倫：你們準備好了嗎？是否要點餐了呢？還是需要再等一下？

**Customer 1 :** We are ready. I'd like a corn chowder and a garden salad.

客人一：我們準備好了。我要一個玉米巧達湯和花園沙拉。

**Allen :** Okay, which **dressing** do you prefer?

艾倫：好的，您想要什麼沙拉醬？

**Customer 1 : Ranch** dressing.

客人一：牧場醬。

**Customer 2 :** Me too. I want extra jalapeño, if it's possible.

客人二：我也一樣，可能的話，請多給我墨西哥辣椒。

**Allen :** All right. We use **Rigatoni** for the macaroni and cheese, just so you to know.

艾倫：沒問題。我們是用水管麵做焗烤通心粉，跟您們說一聲。

**Customer 3 :** Why don't we have a fried **platter**?

客人三：我們何不點個炸物拼盤？

**Allen :** Great idea! We have awesome onion rings and mozzarella sticks.

艾倫：好主意，我們的洋蔥圈和莫札瑞拉起司條很棒呢。

**Customer 1 :** Let's have two platters. And some vegetable sticks, too.

客人一：就點兩個炸物拼盤，還要些蔬菜棒。

**Allen :** No problem. I'll be back later.

艾倫：沒問題。待會兒我會再過來。

**哪裡有問題**

點餐時，因為西方飲食習慣在澱粉和配餐的選擇上比較多，因此最好在最後複誦一遍，好確認餐點都正確無誤。對話中，客人要搭配牧場醬，這是類似亞洲千島醬的一種沙拉醬汁，是非常常見的沙拉醬。另一位顧客則要多一點墨西哥辣椒，這在西方餐廳往往是免費的，其他如多一點起司等要求，雖在亞洲餐廳常要多付費，西方餐廳卻多是免費供應。

# 餐飲補充包

When taking orders, a server needs to be extremely careful **noting down** the items. Not only so, if the dishes are special **in some ways**, it is better to remind the diners. Although it is natural for each restaurant to have their own way of cooking, it is not **considerate** to disappoint **conservative** customers with creative **combinations** or modern cookery.

For instance, mac 'n cheese uses elbow macaroni in the most **classic** way. If the restaurant **employs** another kind of pasta, it will **warm people's heart** by simply telling them. This will **prevent protest** afterwards, too. Some dishes have a higher level of **heat** or spice, and it is not **agreeable** for everyone. Under this circumstance, in order to avoid **unwarned** customers ordering them accidentally, a server is supposed to remind them **in advance**. It is good to and try to reach a **compromise** between the diner's **preference** and the original dish.

# 中譯

點餐時，除了細心記下客人所點的餐點之外，若是餐點有什麼特殊之處，最好也要主動提醒客人。雖然每間餐廳本來就會有自己詮釋餐點的方式，但若因創新的組合或烹調手法，讓守舊或有特殊喜好的客人感到失望或不自在，那就有失考慮。

因此，像焗烤通心粉這種家喻戶曉的菜餚，一般使用迷你通心粉，若是該餐廳使用不同種的義大利麵，則可貼心的通知一聲，避免客人事後抗議。有的菜餚則是在辣度上，不一定適合每一個人，因此若是稍有辣度的菜餚，為避免客人在不知情的情況下點餐，也應該主動告知客人，並在可行的範圍內調整餐點的辣度或調味。

# 字彙和慣用語一覽表

| | | | |
|---|---|---|---|
| dressing | n. 沙拉醬 | ranch | n. 牧場 |
| Rigatoni | 義大利水管麵 | platter | n. 拼盤 |
| note down | 記下 | in some way | 某些方面 |
| considerate | adj. 體貼的 | conservative | adj. 保守的 |
| combination | n. 組合 | classic | adj. 經典的 |
| employ | v. 使用 | warm sb's heart | 使某人感到窩心 |
| prevent | v. 預防 | protest | n. 抗議 |
| heat | n. 辣度 | agreeable | adj. 令人愉快的 |
| unwarned | adj. 不知情的 | in advance | 在…之前 |
| compromise | v. 妥協 | preference | n. 偏好 |

# Unit 1.4 Serving 上餐

Allen / 店員

Customer / 客人

 情境對話  MP3 28

**Allen :** Macaroni and cheese for you.

艾倫：您的焗烤通心粉。

**Customer 2 :** Oh, it's **making my mouth water**.

客人二：噢，真讓我食指大動！

**Allen :** That's a good **sign**. Macaroni and cheese with extra jalapeño.

艾倫：這是好現象。您的特多墨西哥辣椒焗烤通心粉。

**Customer 3 :** Thank you. When it comes to macaroni, the hotter, the better.

客人三：謝謝。說到焗烤通心粉，就是越辣越好吃。

126

**Allen :** Good luck with that! It'll be exciting I bet. Here are your platters and sauces.

**Customer 4 :** Look at the golden crisp on the onion ring. It's perfectly fried without doubt. And look at that size! It's **gigantic**.

**Allen :** Ha-ha, our huge onion rings are well-known. Vegetable sticks too. Chowder and salad for the young lady.

**Customer 1 :** Thank you.

**Allen :** And finally, shrimp scampi. Watch out, ma'am, the plate is **piping** hot. Oh, and there's hot juice in the shrimp. Don't burn yourself.

**Customer 4 :** This is perfect. It smells heavenly.

艾倫：祝好運，我想會很辛辣刺激的。這兒是您們的炸物拼盤和醬汁。

客人四：看看那金黃酥脆的洋蔥圈！不用懷疑，一定炸得恰到好處。還有那個尺寸，真是巨大呀！

艾倫：哈哈，我們的巨大洋蔥圈相當有名呢。蔬菜棒也是，還有年輕小姐的巧達湯和沙拉。

客人一：謝謝你。

艾倫：最後是白酒炒明蝦。請小心，女士，盤子非常燙。噢，蝦子裡有湯汁，小心別燙傷了。

客人四：太棒了，聞起來好香呀。

# 哪裡有問題

上餐時,需要留意的是一定要說出菜名,並輕巧的走至客人桌邊放下。若剛好記得點該道菜的客人,則可以直接放到當事人面前。有的客人會在點餐後忘記自己所點的餐,或是因聊得忘我而忽視服務生上菜的舉動。這時,服務生該有禮的提醒客人,並謹慎的上菜。必要時,也可複誦餐點明細,客人較易想起自己所點的餐。

# 餐飲補充包

Unlike the Taiwanese and the Japanese that treat the customers like gods and being **overly** polite, in western countries, people treat each other rather **equally**. **In other words**, although one is customer and the other is server, constantly repeating "excuse me" is unnecessary, unless the coming dish is a **gratin** or **casserole**. In order to prevent the customer being **burnt** by the dish accidentally, one may **remind** others by saying so. Being a server, one should meet the requirements of serving to the right person, replying properly and being welcoming.

Too many Asian-kinds of polite **greetings**, body **gestures** or even **bowing** may cause **unease** to the guests. When the customers make **remarks** about food, like in the **dialogue**, it is not necessary for a server to join the conversation. Just smile and reply a few words is fine. However, if one is **outgoing**, one may express a **sense of humor** through little **chit-chats**.

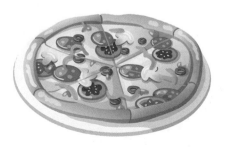

**中譯**

不像台灣、日本等奉客人為至高座上賓、過度有禮的待客方式，歐美國家較有人人平等的感覺。也就是說，雖一方為客，一方為服務員，例如，在上菜時，不需要一直重複「不好意思」，除非是焗烤等連餐盤都很燙的菜餚，為避免在還沒上桌前意外碰到客人的身體，才需要出聲提醒。身為服務生，只要上菜給正確的對象、進退合宜、舉止大方即可。

太多禮貌的詞彙、肢體動作、甚至鞠躬等，都可能造成客人的不自在。若客人就食物發表感想，如對話所示，服務生不一定要做出回應，禮貌性答覆即可。不過，若本身是較為外向的人，也可以跟客人有些幽默的簡短對話。

# 字彙和慣用語一覽表

| | | | |
|---|---|---|---|
| make one's mouth water | 使某人流口水 | sign | n. 跡象 |
| gigantic | adj. 巨大的 | piping | adj. 冒煙的 |
| overly | adv. 過度地 | equally | adv. 平等地 |
| in other words | 換句話說 | gratin | n. 焗烤 |
| casserole | n. 砂鍋料理 | burnt | adj. 燙傷的 |
| remind | v. 提醒 | greeting | n. 招呼 |
| gesture | n. 手勢 | bow | v. 鞠躬 |
| unease | n. 不安 | remark | n. 評論 |
| dialogue | n. 對話 | outgoing | adj. 外向的 |
| sense of humor | 幽默感 | chit-chat | 閒話家常 |

Part

2

餐飲搶分篇

Unit

01

Dining Service 點餐服務及餐間服務

# Service During Meal
# 餐間服務

*Allen* / 店員

*Customer* / 客人

 情境對話

**Allen :** How's everything?

艾倫：一切如何？

**Customer 1 :** It's awesome. My chowder is just the right **thickness** and the salad is fresh.

客人一：很棒，我的巧達湯濃度剛好，沙拉也很新鮮。

**Allen :** That's good to know.

艾倫：真高興妳這麼説。

**Customer 4 :** We really like the platter. You guys **know how to** fry the food.

客人四：我們很喜歡炸物拼盤，你們對油炸真的很有一套呢。

**Allen :** Actually, our chef learned the Japanese

艾倫：其實我們的主廚學到日式天婦羅炸法，並且用在我們的麵

tempura **method** and we used that as our **coating**. Maybe that's why. It's lighter and less greasy.

衣上。可能這就是原因所在，炸物比較清爽不油膩。

**Customer 4 :** That's **innovative**. It really works, and it's delicious.

客人四：真是創新呀，很有效果，也很好吃。

**Allen :** Can I get you more water? Maybe a beer or something?

艾倫：您們需要加水嗎？還是要啤酒之類的？

**Customer 3 :** Yeah, I'd like another electric mojito, please.

客人三：嗯，請再給我一杯電擊薄荷調酒。

**Allen :** Yeah, it cleans your **palate**, too. What about the ladies? Some water?

艾倫：是呀，這款調酒會清味蕾。女士們如何呢？需要水嗎？

**Customer 1 :** I'll have an iced tea. Thank you.

客人一：我想來杯冰茶，謝謝。

**Allen :** I'll be right back.

艾倫：馬上來。

**哪裡有問題**

點餐、上餐到結帳之間，服務生並非呆站或專注於服務新客人。

在客人買單之前，服務生必須每隔數分鐘便觀察、問候一下該桌的客人。

加水、加點飲料的服務是最常見的，若是餐點有問題，例如食物不夠熱、或其他對餐點不滿意而要退回食物時，也會在這時候反應。

若非難以忍受的嚴重問題，客人通常是不會主動離席去找服務生的，而這也是餐後會給予小費的原因。

# 餐飲補充包

After the meals are served, a server has to **keep an eye on** the table. Of course, no one wants to be **disturbed** by a **bugging** server during a fabulous dinner. Hence, a server needs to **cultivate** the sense of proper **timing**; one should be **caring** yet not overly disturbing.

In general, when a server is walking around collecting plates, one should look around to make sure everything is in shape. If the customers have had an empty glass for a while, it's time for a server to **come up** and offer to **refill** the water or take **further** beverage **orders**.

Even if there's nothing special, **during the whole time** the customers are dining a server needs to come up twice at least twice. They do this to greet, to ask if everything is **satisfying**, and to offer other services. The tip that a server receives will depend on the **diligence** with which one **performs** during the meal. It can go from 10% to **up to** 20% (in the U.S.).

**中譯**

當上菜完畢後，服務生需不時關注該桌的狀況。當然，沒有人希望在用餐期間不斷被煩人的服務生打擾，因此如何適時的上前問候，卻不致於讓人感覺受到打岔，是服務生必須培養出來的感知力。

一般而言，當服務生來回走動，收走各桌的杯盤時，就應該四處觀察是否有異。若發現客人杯子空了一段時間，便可以主動上前詢問加水、加點飲料的服務。

就算完全沒有狀況，在客人用餐期間，服務生最少也要上前詢問兩次，關心客人對食物的滿意程度，或是否需要其他服務。服務生會依據用餐期間的殷勤程度，收到 10%～20%不等的小費（以美國的狀況而言）。

# 字彙和慣用語一覽表

| | | | |
|---|---|---|---|
| thickness | n. 濃稠度 | sb knows how to... | 做…很有一套 |
| method | n. 方法 | coating | n. 麵衣 |
| innovative | adj. 創新的 | palate | n. 味蕾 |
| keep an eye on | 留心 | disturb | v. 打擾 |
| bugging | adj. 煩人的 | cultivate | v. 培養 |
| timing | n. 時機 | caring | adj. 關心的 |
| come up | 上前 | refill | v. 再注入 |
| further order | 加點 | during the whole time | 在…的整個期間 |
| satisfying | adj. 使人滿意的 | diligence | n. 殷勤 |
| perform | v. 表現出 | up to | 高達 |

# Unit 1.6 Paying 買單

Allen / 店員

Customer / 客人

 情境對話

 MP3 30

**Customer 1 :** I think we are **all set**. Let's call the waiter.

客人一：我想我們該走了，叫服務生過來吧。

**Customer 2 :** Excuse me, can we have the **bill** please?

客人二：不好意思，請給我們帳單。

**Allen :** You are good? No dessert? Anything else?

艾倫：您們結束了嗎？需不需要甜點或其他東西呢？

**Customer 3 :** Thank you. It was delicious, but we are **stuffed**.

客人三：謝謝，東西都很好吃，但我們已經吃飽了。

**Allen : Sure thing**. Do you want to **split** the bill or pay altogether?

艾倫：沒問題，您們想要分開結帳還是一起結？

**Customer 3 :** We'd like to have separate bills. Thanks.

客人三：我們希望分開結帳，謝謝。

**Allen : No sweat**, sir.

艾倫：好的。

**Customer 3 :** There you go.

客人三：拿去吧。

**Allen :** Okay, let me get the **change** for you.

艾倫：好的，我去找錢給您。

**Customer 3 :** That's okay. You can keep it.

客人三：不必了，剩下的是小費。

**Allen : Why**, thank you! Please sign here, and I'll take care of the rest.

艾倫：噢，謝謝，請在這兒簽名就可以了。

**Customer 4 :** Tonight was wonderful. Thanks for everything. This is a great place.

客人四：今晚真的很棒。謝謝你的服務，這是間好餐廳。

**Allen :** You are welcome. Have a good night.

艾倫：不客氣，祝您有美好的夜晚。

**哪裡有問題**

結帳代表用餐的時刻結束，也代表服務生的工作告一段
落。在美國，結帳分為信用卡及現金兩種，差別僅在於
一個需要簽名，一個不用，所應支付的小費都是相同
的。在一些等級較模糊的餐館，例如提供雞尾酒的披薩
店、酒館等地方，服務生較不會期待收到小費，這時若
覺得服務生的態度好，可以直接在付現時請對方不必找
零，表示剩下的錢是對方的小費。

# 餐飲補充包

When the customers ask for bill, it doesn't **necessarily** mean that they are leaving, but it **indicates** that they no longer need the server's attention. From the point on, even if the customers have an empty glass, it's not a server's **responsibility** to be as **attentive** as before.

Bill-paying can be **individually** or **all-at-once**. After the bill **is handed to** the customer, they will need a few moments to decide how much they are going to leave for tips. The cash or card will be **folded** in the bill **wallet** and a server may take back the wallet. Every bill that's in the wallet is for the server, and **there's no need to** return and **ask for** tips.

Sometimes, if a customer **feels like** leaving more tips after the wallet is taken away, one may just put the cash on the table and leave.

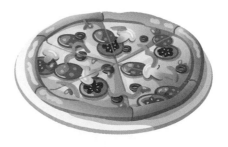

# 中譯

當客人要求結帳時，並不代表他們立刻就要離開，但這代表他們不再需要服務生的服務了。從付帳的時候起，就算客人的杯子空了，也不再是服務生的責任，當然也不需要殷勤的問候。

付帳時可以分開算或一起結帳，當帳單交到客人手上後，他們會需要一點時間來決定要給服務生多少小費。現金或信用卡會直接夾在帳單皮套裡，服務生只需要拿回帳單皮套即可。所有在皮套裡的鈔票都是要給服務生的，因此不需要再回去要小費。

有時候，若是顧客在交出帳單皮套後，還想要留下更多小費，便會直接將現金放在桌上並離席。

# 字彙和慣用語一覽表

| | | | |
|---|---|---|---|
| all set | 準備好了 | bill | n. 帳單 |
| stuffed | adj. 飽脹的 | sure thing | =sure |
| split | v. 分開 | no sweat | 不客氣 |
| change | n. 找零 | why,… | =well, …噢 |
| necessarily | adv. 一定 | indicate | v. 表示 |
| responsibility | n. 責任 | attentive | adj. 留意的 |
| individually | adv. 個別地 | all-at-once | adj. 一次的 |
| be handed to | 交給 | fold | v. 夾 |
| wallet | n. 皮套 | there's no need to | （某事）是不必要的 |
| ask for | 要求 | feel like | 想要 |

143

# Reservation
## 訂位

*Allen* / 店員

*Customer* / 客人

 **情境對話**

**Customer :** Hi, I'd like to make a **reservation** for two, Saturday evening, at 6 o'clock.

客人：您好，我想訂兩個位子，週六下午六點。

**Allen :** Right, just a moment please. Ma'am, I'm sorry, but we are **packed** on Saturday night.

艾倫：好的，請稍等。女士，不好意思，我們週六晚上已經預約滿了。

**Customer :** Oh, I didn't **see that coming**. The whole night is **booked**? What about 7:30 or 8 o'clock?

客人：噢，真想不到。整個晚上都滿了嗎？七點半或八點呢？

**Allen :** I'm very sorry Ma'am, but I'm afraid we have a **full house** throughout Saturday evening.

艾倫：真的很抱歉，但是我們週六是客滿的。

**Customer :** Alright. What about Sunday evening?

客人：好，那星期日晚上呢？

**Allen :** That works. Sunday evening at 6 o'clock, two people?

艾倫：可以，星期日晚上六點，兩位嗎？

**Customer :** That's correct. I'd like to sit on the **patio**, if it is **available**.

客人：沒錯，我想訂陽台的位子，如果可以的話。

**Allen :** Patio seat, I got it. Your name and number please?

艾倫：陽台的位子，我記下了，請給我您的名字和電話。

**Customer :** Charlene Brown, 1-604-228-8224.

客人：查爾斯布朗，1-60-42-28-82-24。

**Allen :** Okay, Ma'am. You're all set.

艾倫：好的，這樣就行了。

**Customer :** Thanks a lot.

客人：謝謝你。

 **哪裡有問題**

顧客來電訂位時，艾倫發現他要訂的時間已經沒有空位了。通常，若是店內狀況無法配合客人預定的時間，只要委婉說明即可，毋須多做其他解釋。若是客人自行更改時間，則須確定來店的人數、時間，及客人的特殊要求，例如文中的陽台座等。留下客人的姓名、稱謂及聯絡方式也是相當重要的，一般餐廳常有保留位子十分鐘的規定，以免客人沒有依約出現。

# 餐飲補充包

When someone makes a reservation, it is necessary to **confirm** the number of people, arriving time and contact methods. Leaving contact methods not only **provides** a way to **deal with** not-on-time customers, but is also a way for the restaurant to **inform** their guests when there are any **unexpected** problems.

If the staff are considerate, they should ask about any special events, such as a **proposal**, birthday celebration, **anniversary** celebration, etc. **Putting out** proper celebration cards and cakes, **as long as** it doesn't disturb other customers, is a great way to give good service.

Generally speaking, **outdoor** seats and patio seats are for customers that smoke. In European countries, people like to sit in the patio where they can have **air flow** and a good view. Thus, without a reservation, it can be hard to get these seats. The staff members that take phone calls need to pay attention to these details in order to avoid **arguments** or any **misunderstandings**.

**中譯**

客人以電話訂位時，需確認來客總人數、抵達時間及聯絡方式。留下客人的聯絡方式不但是預防客人在預約時間沒出現的問題，也幫助餐廳在有突發狀況時，能及時通知每一位訂位的客人。

若是接電話的工作人員體貼，則能詢問顧客是否有任何特殊活動，例如客人要求婚、慶祝生日、紀念日等，並在不妨礙其他客人的情況下，送上適當的小立牌或蛋糕等，都是餐廳重視客人的表現。

一般來說，餐廳的戶外座或露天座是提供給需吸菸的客人，但是在歐洲國家，許多人喜歡坐在通風、視野好的陽台座，因此若非先訂位，這些位子是一位難求的。負責訂位的人需留意這些細節，以避免事後糾紛或誤解。

# 字彙和慣用語一覽表

| reservation | v. 預約 | packed | adj. 客滿的 |
|---|---|---|---|
| see sth. coming | 預料某事 | booked | adj. 預訂的 |
| full house | 客滿 | patio | n. 露臺 |
| available | adj. 可取得的 | confirm | v. 確認 |
| provide | v. 提供 | deal with | 應付 |
| inform | v. 告知 | unexpected | adj. 無預期的 |
| proposal | n. 求婚 | anniversary | n. 周年 |
| put out | 擺出 | as long as | 只要 |
| outdoor | adj. 戶外的 | air flow | 通風 |
| argument | n. 爭執 | misunderstanding | n. 誤解 |

 Allen / 店員

 Customer / 客人

 **情境對話**　　　　

**Allen :** Hello, this is Classic American.

艾倫：嗨，這裡是經典小美式。

**Customer :** Hi, I've heard that your restaurant features **family-style** cooking. May I ask what's on your menu?

客人：嗨，我聽說你們的店是以家庭風格的料理為特色，我能問問菜單上有什麼嗎？

**Allen :** Oh, we have many items. Do you want to know anything **specific**? Appetizers, **entrées** or …?

艾倫：噢，我們有許多品項。您有特別想問的嗎？開胃菜、主菜或…？

**Customer :** What do you have for entrées?

客人：你們有什麼主菜？

**Allen :** We have the classic American burger; it's made with home **cured** bacon, sautéed mushrooms and American cheese. The burger is served with home fries. Our soup is pretty good, too. We have cauliflower soup and leek and potato soup.

**Customer :** Sounds great. What else do you have?

**Allen :** Well, I'd say our meatloaf is pretty **badass**. We make it daily and serve it with homemade red sauce, not just normal ketchup. Also we serve it with freshly **tossed** garden salad.

**Customer :** Wow, it's pretty appetizing just to hear about it. Thank you very much.

**Allen :** Pleasure, ma'am, **anytime**. **Have a good one**.

艾倫：我們有經典美式漢堡，由自家煙燻培根、炒蘑菇和美國起司製成，附上自家製薯條。我們的湯也很不錯，有花椰菜濃湯和大蔥馬鈴薯濃湯。

客人：聽起來真棒，其他還有什麼呢？

艾倫：我們的肉派也很好吃。每天新鮮現做，佐以自製紅醬，不是普通番茄醬，並附上現拌的沙拉。

客人：哇，聽起來真令人食指大動。謝謝你的介紹。

艾倫：不客氣，女士，隨時歡迎。祝您有美好的一天。

# 哪裡有問題

不論是曾前去用餐過的客人，或是完全沒去過店裡消費的客人，都有可能打電話來詢問菜單。因為講電話的時間有限，若是接到主動詢問的電話，最好不要把菜單從頭到尾說過一遍，而是挑推薦菜色介紹即可。推薦菜色可能是自己喜歡的料理、也可能實際一點，就推薦店裡最貴的餐點。要怎麼推薦端看店員本身的判斷，但推薦得引人食慾是成功的要領。

# 餐飲補充包

When a customer first comes in a restaurant, the **recommendation** of the server is usually required. The same thing happens on the phone. Curious customers get to know the menu and the **image** of the restaurant through the phone. The staff members that answer **represent** the restaurant. Through his or her reply, people will **form** a **first impression** of the restaurant. This might **determine** whether they come to eat or not, so the staff's response and **attitude** are quite **crucial**. If the staff is not **passionate** about the menu, he or she will not be able to recommend anything **sincerely**. On the other hand, if the staff of the restaurant are very confident in their food, it speaks well about the menu. Instead of recommending something in an **automatic** way, introducing the dishes that one really likes is way better. However, it is a **must** to meet the customers' special needs, such as wanting soup, not wanting to eat fried food, of trying to eat healthier, just to name a few.

**中譯**

初次到店內消費的客人，常會請店員推薦菜單，而在電話中也是一樣，好奇的顧客透過電話認識餐廳的菜單及該店的形象。店員在電話中代表了餐廳，透過他的介紹，餐廳的風格、第一印象也因而定案，甚至決定客人是否光顧餐廳。因此，店員在電話中的反應及態度是相當重要的。若是店員對菜單缺乏熱情，便無法真誠的推薦料理；反之，若店員對自家餐點很有自信，在語氣中便會傳達給顧客。與其官方、制式化的推薦店內人氣菜餚，不如將自己真心喜歡的料理推薦給顧客。若是客人有特殊需求，例如想喝湯品、不吃油炸等，則需按照客人的需求推薦店內的餐點。

# 字彙和慣用語一覽表

| | | | |
|---|---|---|---|
| family-style | adj. 家庭式的 | specific | adj. 特定的 |
| entrée | n. 主菜 | cure | v. 燻製 |
| badass | 狠角色 | toss | v. 拌 |
| anytime | 沒問題、不客氣（放在句尾） | have a good one | =have a good day |
| recommendation | n. 推薦 | image | n. 形象 |
| represent | v. 代表 | form | v. 成形 |
| first impression | 第一印象 | determine | v. 決定 |
| attitude | n. 態度 | crucial | adj. 關鍵的 |
| passionate | adj. 熱情的 | sincerely | adv. 真誠地 |
| automatic | adj. 自動的 | must | n. 必要的事物 |

# Pickup Order
# 外帶點餐

Allen / 店員    Customer / 客人    Jeremy / 股東

 ## 情境對話

**Customer :** Hello, is this Classic American?

客人：您好，請問是經典小美式嗎？

**Allen :** Hi, what can I do for you?

艾倫：您好，我能為您做什麼呢？

**Customer :** I'd like to place a pickup order please.

客人：我想外帶點餐。

**Allen :** Of course. You can go ahead.

艾倫：沒問題，您請說。

**Customer :** I'd like calamari for an appetizer, two **bourbon** burgers, one **filet**

客人：我要一個炸花枝開胃菜、兩個波本漢堡、一道腓力牛排、一個塔可餅三重奏、還有玉米濃

**mignon**, one taco **trio**, and one corn chowder. Oh, and a big Caesar salad.

**Allen :** What would you like for the side dishes for the filet mignon? We have onion rings, fries, squash **puree**…

**Customer :** Onion rings and squash please. As for the fries for the burgers, can I have one normal fries and one sweet potato fries?

**Allen :** No problem. Anything else?

**Customer :** And I'd like to have all fish tacos with **crema** sauce, spicy **salsa** on the side.

**Allen :** All noted, ma'am. Your meal will be ready in 30 minutes.

**Customer :** I'll be there.

湯。噢，我還要一個加大的凱薩沙拉。

艾倫：腓力牛排的配菜您想要什麼呢？我們有洋蔥圈、薯條、南瓜泥…

客人：請給我洋蔥圈和南瓜泥。另外，漢堡的薯條我想換成地瓜薯條，可以嗎？

艾倫：當然沒問題，還有什麼需要嗎？

客人：塔可餅請都做成炸魚配奶油醬，辣味莎莎醬另外放。

艾倫：都記下了，女士。您的餐點會在三十分鐘後做好。

客人：我會準時去拿的。

# 哪裡有問題

文中的客人用電話點餐，並會在稍後前去取餐。這是一種方便的點餐模式，讓客人不用親自到場，且能在餐點準備好後直接取回，相當省時。因為西餐的附餐眾多，像是漢堡、三明治類一定會附薯條，排餐則會有蔬菜和炸物的附餐等，許多的細節需要在電話中詳細確認。另外，像薯條換地瓜薯、凱薩沙拉加大等，通常都是要多付費的，這些則不需要在電話中特別說明。

# 餐飲補充包

Usually, if a restaurant has a takeout service, they will offer pickup orders as well. All the orders for entrées, side dishes, beverages are taken in one phone call, and picking them up later in the restaurant is a time-saving and convenient method.

However, for a restaurant, there is a **risk** for a pickup order. If the customers don't **show up**, the food will become wasted. To prevent this from happening, the staff member that answers the phone needs to carefully take the names and contact numbers of the customers, and tell them the **approximate** waiting time.

The staff member should also remind them to come in **on time**. When the items for a pickup order are **numerous**, the staff must count everything: entrées, side dishes, and sauces, all packed up separately in takeout boxes. If the customers find anything missing after they leave, **normally** they won't return to complain. Yet, that **reveals** the **failure** of the staff, so it is better to pay extra attention to this.

# 中譯

通常只要餐廳提供外帶服務，都會附帶提供電話點餐外帶。一通電話交代所有主餐、附餐、飲品，並在稍後前去取餐，這是非常省時、方便的做法。

然而，對餐廳而言，這樣的作法卻有風險。若是客人遲遲不現身，將造成食材的浪費。為避免這樣的情形，接電話的員工需注意，確認留下客人的姓名及聯絡方式後，記得告知大約等待的時間，並叮嚀客人務必準時前來領餐。

而對餐廳服務人員來說，若是客人點的品項多，需一一清點主餐、附餐、各種醬汁，並分門別類裝入外帶盒中。若是客人在離開後才發現品項有少，通常不會再回到餐廳反應，然而這樣卻顯示出工作人員的粗心，因此須特別留意。

# 字彙和慣用語一覽表

| bourbon | n. 波本威士忌 | filet mignon | n. 腓力牛排 |
|---|---|---|---|
| trio | n. 三個 | puree | n. 菜泥 |
| crema | n. 墨西哥奶油醬 | salsa | n. 莎莎醬 |
| risk | n. 風險 | show up | 現身 |
| approximate | adj. 大約的 | on time | 準時 |
| numerous | adj. 眾多的 | normally | adv. 一般來說 |
| reveal | v. 揭示 | failure | n. 失敗 |

補充字彙

| T-bone | 丁骨牛排 | New York Strip | 紐約客牛排 |
|---|---|---|---|
| Ribeye | 肋眼牛排 | tortilla | 墨西哥薄餅 |
| guacamole | 墨西哥酪梨醬 | quesadilla | 中間夾起司的墨西哥薄餅 |

# Reserved for Private Use
# 聚餐包場

*Allen* / 店員

*Customer* / 客人

 情境對話

**Allen :** Hi, Classic American.

艾倫：嗨，這裡是經典小美式。

**Customer :** Hello, I've been to your place, and I loved it. Wonderful **atmosphere**, great staff, delicious food.

客人：您好，我去過貴餐廳，覺得很喜歡。氣氛佳、工作人員和善、食物又好吃。

**Allen :** Thank you! I'm glad we have satisfied you.

艾倫：謝謝您，很高興我們令您滿意。

**Customer :** So I'm thinking, is it possible to **reserve** one whole night for a **private** party? It's a **tiny** wedding celebration, just family

客人：我在想，有沒有可能包下整晚當作派對場地呢？我們有個迷你婚禮，只有家庭成員和一些朋友，但我想包全場。

members and some friends, but I'd like to reserve the whole place.

**Allen :** Oh! What's the date, please?

**Customer :** It's on May 9<sup>th</sup>.

艾倫：噢！請問是幾月幾號呢？

客人：五月九號。

**Allen :** Okay. We have to **calculate** the **estimated** fee, and later I'll get back to you. We will take half of the total **fee** in advance, is that **acceptable** for you?

艾倫：好的。我們必須估計費用，待會兒我再回撥給您。我們必須事先收取一半的費用，您可以接受嗎？

**Customer :** I'm **cool with it**. About the menu, we would like to talk in the store.

客人：沒問題。至於菜單，我們想在店裡討論。

**Allen :** Awesome. Our manager Jeremy will be expecting you. Thanks for choosing us.

艾倫：太棒了，傑瑞米經理會等候您來。謝謝您選擇我們。

# 哪裡有問題

客人想包場進行派對活動時，餐廳方面會先收取場地費，接著再依照菜單、需提供的特別服務等另外收費。一般來說，包場服務僅限定於特定人數以上的客人，或是因為活動特殊，餐廳較可能破例接受包場。一般來說，店東都會為自己訂下包場服務的最低人數。剛成為餐飲新鮮人時，不妨問問老闆這方面的限制，避免自己妄下決定，或冒失回答客人。

# 餐飲補充包

Common private events, including wedding parties, birthday parties, school **reunions**, school club gatherings, etc. If the customers don't **fancy** catering or are not comfortable with it, that is when they may come to a restaurant and reserve it for private use.

Generally speaking, only the owner of the restaurant or **authorized** floor managers can decide whether they accept a private reservation. Because **profits** need to **remain** high, the owner has a big decision to make when it comes to closing for a private party. Besides **venue fees**, there are usually customized food that corresponds to the event. For example, in a steak house, the food is usually served in smaller portions and with more **varieties**.

Another case: in a wedding party, the **provider** needs to have finger food so that the customers can enjoy standing and walking around. Alcohol is also served in this **occasion**. The owner or the manager will decide the customized menu after they discuss with the **representative** of the event, then explain the **operation** to the whole staff.

## 中譯

常見的餐廳包場活動有：婚禮宴會、生日派對、同學會、迎新送舊…等。若客人不想以外燴形式慶祝，多直接借用餐廳場地進行活動。

一般來說，餐廳是否提供包場，完全是由店主人決定，或是由店主授權經理決定。因為包場涉及的問題較多，若是沒有一定的收益，一般來說並不會主動提供此項服務。包場除了需付場地費之外，通常也會有因應活動而產生的餐點。在以排餐為主的餐廳，常會以多樣、小份的方式，讓每位客人品嘗到多樣美食。

若是婚禮慶祝等熱鬧的場合，則會提供能讓賓客站著享用的手指美食，並搭配酒類飲品等。如何客製化餐點，會在店主或經理與包場負責人討論後，再轉達給所有餐廳工作人員。

# 字彙和慣用語一覽表

| | | | |
|---|---|---|---|
| atmosphere | n. 氣氛 | reserve | v. 預約 |
| private | adj. 私人的 | tiny | adj. 迷你的 |
| calculate | v. 計算 | estimate | v. 估計 |
| fee | n. 費用 | acceptable | adj. 可接受的 |
| cool with sth. | 對某事感到同意 | reunion | n. 重聚 |
| fancy | v. 愛好 | authorize | v. 授權 |
| profit | n. 收益 | remain | v. 仍是 |
| venue fee | n. 場地費 | variety | n. 多樣 |
| provider | n. 供應商 | occasion | n. 場合 |
| representative | n. 代表 | operation | n. 運作 |

# Customized Meal
# 客製化餐點

*Allen* / 店員

*Customer* / 客人

 **情境對話**

 MP3 35

**Customer :** I'd like to place a pickup order please.

客人：我想外帶點餐。

**Allen :** You can go ahead.

艾倫：請説。

**Customer :** I'd like to have a seafood bake. But I am wondering if you could **switch** the shrimp in there for something else? **Bass**, **haddock** or something.

客人：我要一個海鮮焗烤盅，不過我在想，是否可以將蝦子換成其他食材呢？例如鱸魚、黑線鱈之類的。

**Allen :** Sure! That's no problem. Are you **allergic** to shrimp? We can cook

艾倫：當然可以，沒問題。您對蝦過敏嗎？我們可以另外烹調。

the food separately for you.

**Customer :** Yes, I am. Thank you so much.

客人：正是如此，非常謝謝你。

**Allen :** Anything else?

艾倫：還需要什麼嗎？

**Customer :** I'd like to have a chocolate French toast, too. But I don't like the **condensed milk** on there… can I change it to the normal maple **syrup**?

客人：我想要一個巧克力法式吐司。不過，可以把上面淋的煉乳換成普通楓糖漿嗎？

**Allen :** You got it. Is it too sweet for you?

艾倫：可以，對您來說太甜了是嗎？

**Customer :** No, just **lactose intolerant**. That's all I need.

客人：不，只是乳糖不耐症。這樣就好。

**Allen :** You're all set, ma'am. Please come by in 40 minutes.

艾倫：全記下了。請在四十分鐘後過來。

# 哪裡有問題

對話中，客人因為自己對蝦子過敏及患有乳糖不耐症，便要求工作人員幫他的餐點作微調。在西方，常遇到客人要求食物中無奶、無蛋或無麵粉，因為膽固醇、過敏等問題嚴重，若餐廳不懂得臨機應變，將會失去很多客人。在前面的對話中，僅僅是將煉乳換成楓糖漿，並非太大的調整，但若是製作料理根本上的調整，就需要先徵詢廚房意見再下決定了。

# 餐飲補充包

**Adjusting** the menu **subtly** for customers is not only a way to impress them, but a responsibility for a good business. Just like in Asian society, it is quite common to see people **request** special orders for their meals. From the method of cooking the vegetables, to the sauce on a dish, the customers communicate with the owners and staff of the business all the time.

The same thing happens among Westerners. For instance, a breakfast diner often makes egg whites omelet for those who seek for lower calories, and this corresponds to the fear for **cholesterol** of modern people as well. Not only that, it is also common to see people asking for salad instead of fries for their side dish, in order to lower their **grease intake**.

Customizing a meal is an important task for the server and **involves** the cooks. If a server is not certain about the kitchen details, they should first confirm with the kitchen, then give out a response **based on** the food **inventory** and the **abilities** of the kitchen staff to meets the request.

**中譯**

適度的依來客要求調整餐點，不僅是讓客人留下好印象的作法，更是考驗餐廳在經營及實行上的成熟度。就像華人社會中，也常見對餐點有特殊要求一樣，從青菜的烹調方式到淋的醬汁，客人都能跟店家做溝通。

在西方社會也是如此。舉例來說，一般的早午餐店家就常因客人要求，而使用純蛋白製作煎蛋捲。如此不僅取悅了想降低熱量攝取的客人，也順應現代人擔心膽固醇的問題。另外，也常見客人要求將附餐薯條改成沙拉，藉此降低餐點的油膩程度。

客製化餐點常是與顧客面對面時碰到的難題，若是不確定是否在實行上可行，則應先徵詢廚房的意見後，再依照餐廳的食材庫存、廚師能力等條件，回應客人的要求。

# 字彙和慣用語一覽表

| | | | |
|---|---|---|---|
| switch | v. 替換 | bass | n. 鱸魚 |
| haddock | n. 黑線鱈 | allergic | adj. 過敏的 |
| condensed milk | n. 煉乳 | syrup | n. 糖漿 |
| lactose | n. 乳糖 | intolerance | n. 不耐 |
| adjust | v. 調整 | subtly | adj. 巧妙的 |
| request | v. 要求 | cholesterol | n. 膽固醇 |
| grease | n. 油脂 | intake | n. 攝取 |
| involve | v. 涵蓋 | base on | 基於 |
| inventory | n. 庫存 | ability | n. 能力 |

補充字彙

| | | | |
|---|---|---|---|
| diabetes | 糖尿病 | gluten | 麩質 |

# Unit 3.1

# Opening Hours
# 營業時間

 Allen / 店員　　 Customer / 客人　　 Jeremy / 股東

 **情境對話**

**Allen :** Classic American, how can I help you?

艾倫：經典小美式，請問您需要什麼？

**Customer :** Hi, I'd like to know your **operating** hours please?

客人：嗨，我想請問貴店的營業時間。

**Allen :** We are open from 6am to 12pm Wednesday through Friday. On weekends we are open until 9pm.

艾倫：我們從週三到週五都是從早上六點營業到中午十二點，週末則是營業到晚上九點。

**Customer :** Perfect! I just want to know is it possible

客人：太好了！我還想請問貴店在打烊後，是否還能繼續坐一下

174

to stay a little bit longer after you're closed? Just **in case**.

**Allen :** Can I **get back to** you later? I need to ask our owner.

**Allen :** How should I respond, Jeremy?

**Jeremy :** Of course, they can stay a little bit longer. We have to clean up **and stuff**, so they can be here for another half an hour, if they want.

**Allen :** But no more orders?

**Jeremy :** That's correct. I understand some people would like to **chill** and just **lay back** in a diner, and it's okay with us.

呢？我想先問問看。

艾倫：我待會回撥給您好嗎？我需要跟老闆確認。

艾倫：傑瑞米，我該怎麼回答？

傑瑞米：客人當然是可以再坐一會兒，我們還需要打掃環境之類的，所以他們想的話，可以再留個三十分鐘。

艾倫：但是不能再點餐。

傑瑞米：正是。我了解有些人想在餐廳坐著消磨時間，對我們來說沒什麼大礙。

# 哪裡有問題

餐廳打烊後，要不要請客人離開？這是很多餐廳都會遇到的問題，通常若非有特別註明，一家餐廳的營業時間等於出餐時間，過了這段時段就不再接受點餐。但若是客人想慢慢享用他們的餐點，以致超過店家營業時間，若店主許可，是不需要特別請客人離開的。現在追求「翻桌率」的店家越來越多，有用餐時間限制的店也跟著增加，因此這方面的資訊對客人來說相當重要。

# 餐飲補充包

It's common to receive calls **inquiring** about hours of operation in a restaurant. The hours depend **thoroughly** on the type of restaurant. In western countries, there are **roughly** two kinds of restaurants, one is the family-style diner which contains 30~50 seats normally. This kind of restaurants are usually **casual** and **approachable**, yet the customers don't **tend to** stay inside after the restaurants are closed.

The other is a **chain** restaurant or **commercial** restaurant which **contains** more than 100 seats. There is usually a bar in this type of restaurant, and since the bar is the most **profitable** part of the business, they usually run until late at night. Often, they allow the customers to chat and drink as long as they want.

This type of restaurant doesn't have **strict** closing hours, so it's more tiring to work in there. However, longer hours mean more **tips**. It's better to **think twice** before **applying to** this kind of restaurant.

**中譯**

在餐廳工作，很常接到詢問營業時間的電話，而這完全依該店的性質而定。歐美的餐廳主要分成兩類，一種是家庭經營的餐館，座位 30～50 個左右，通常感覺輕鬆、溫馨，但是餐廳打烊後客人不能久坐。

另一種是座位數超過 100 個的連鎖或商業餐廳，通常這種店都有吧檯，而因為吧檯是整間餐廳最賺錢的部分，通常不是營業到深夜，就是任由顧客在用餐完繼續喝酒聊天。

這種店家較不會有嚴格的打烊時間，因此在這種餐廳工作也會比較累。雖說如此，工作越晚，小費也可能越多，因此最好考慮清楚後，再去應徵這類餐廳。

# 字彙和慣用語一覽表

| | | | |
|---|---|---|---|
| operate | v. 營業 | in case | 以防萬一 |
| get back to sb. | 回覆（人） | …and stuff | 之類的 |
| chill | 消磨時間、鬼混 | lay back | 放鬆 |
| inquire | v. 詢問 | thoroughly | adv. 透徹地 |
| roughly | adv. 粗略地 | casual | adj. 非正式的 |
| approachable | adj. 可親近的 | tend to | 傾向於 |
| chain | n. 連鎖 | commercial | adj. 商業的 |
| contain | v. 包含 | profitable | adj. 有利可圖的 |
| strict | adj. 嚴格的 | tip | n. 小費 |
| think twice | 三思而行 | apply to | 應徵 |

 Allen / 店員　 Customer / 客人　Jeremy / 股東

 ## 情境對話
MP3 37

**Customer :** Hi, we are on our way to your restaurant, but we can't find it. Could you tell me how to get there using **route** 1?

**Allen :** Of course. Do you see a gas station on your right side? From there, go on route 1 for two **miles**. Turn left. There will be a Dollar Tree on your left hand side. Go for another ten minutes, and we are on your right.

客人：嗨，我們正在前往貴餐廳的路上，但是找不到餐廳位置。您能告訴我該怎麼從一號公路前往餐廳嗎？

艾倫：當然。您有在右手邊看到加油站嗎？從那兒起，在一號公路上直走兩英里，之後左轉。在您左手邊會看到百元商店，再繼續走十分鐘後，餐廳會出現在您右手邊。

**Customer :** Thanks. Hope we will be there soon.

客人：謝謝，希望我們很快就能到達。

**Allen :** Why do so many people **have problems finding** our restaurant?

艾倫：為什麼這麼多人都找不到我們餐廳呢？

**Jeremy :** Because we are not on the main road; we are a country-style restaurant after all.

傑瑞米：因為我們不在主要道路上，畢竟我們是鄉村風餐廳。

**Allen :** Couldn't we print out driving directions on our **business card**?

艾倫：我們不能在餐廳名片上印交通路線圖嗎？

**Jeremy :** That won't be necessary. People **nowadays rely on** the Internet more than on paper cards. Plus, there are driving **directions** on our website.

傑瑞米：不需要，現代人依賴網路的程度遠勝於紙卡，更何況我們網站上的確有交通路線圖。

**Allen :** I guess you are right.

艾倫：我想你說的有理。

 **哪裡有問題**

對話中,艾倫對客人總是打電話來詢問交通路線感到有點困擾,便詢問傑瑞米是否可以在名片上印交通路線圖。在名片上印住址及交通路線,對台灣的餐廳來說是相當常見的舉動,然而歐美的餐廳卻不一定如此。一般而言,歐美的餐廳不一定會有名片,就算有,頂多也僅有住址、電話等,不會像台灣的餐廳印上豐富的資訊。

# 餐飲補充包

Working in a restaurant, phone calls requiring driving directions are **inevitable**. As a **local**, these questions should be nothing but **a piece of cake**, yet for **short-term part-timers**, this could be **a pain in the neck**. Take the United States for example, **generally speaking**, there is a main road that goes through every town. Starting the directions by pointing out the main road will **reduce** the chance of getting lost.

Miles are used as the distance **unit** in the States. Hence, driving for how many miles and for how long is common **estimations** for car drivers. Besides the name of the road, marks on the side of the road are used for turns. For instance, fast food restaurants and gas stations are both commonly **spotted** on the main road. Usually, in a **vast** country, cars are the only transportation.

Even if one doesn't drive himself, it is better to be familiar with the name of the roads and traffic directions, so that one won't be **embarrassed** in responding to customers' calls.

Part 2 餐飲搶分篇

Unit 03 Q&A on the Phone 電話詢問

**中譯**

在餐廳工作時,難免會接到詢問交通資訊的電話。若是在當地生活已久,要指路想必不成問題,但若是在國外短期遊學打工者,這問題可能就有點棘手了。以美國為例,一般小鎮上都會有條貫穿全鎮的主要道路,以這條道路為指標,迷路的機會相當低。

美國使用英里為距離單位,因此開車幾英里、幾分鐘是汽車駕駛常用來衡量距離的說法。除了路名之外,也可利用大型路標作為轉彎處的指示,例如速食店、加油站等,都是主要道路上非常常見的路標。

因為在地大的國家,汽車常是唯一的交通方式,因此就算自己本身不開車,還是要對路名、路線等多加熟悉,才能在遇到問題時順利回答。

# 字彙和慣用語一覽表

| | | | |
|---|---|---|---|
| route | n. 路線 | mile | n. 英里 |
| have problem doing sth. | 做某事有困難 | business card | n. 名片 |
| nowadays | adv. 如今 | rely on | 依靠 |
| direction | n. 方向 | inevitable | adj. 不可避免的 |
| local | n. 當地人 | a piece of cake | 易如反掌之事 |
| short-term | adj. 短期的 | part-timer | n. 打工者 |
| a pain in the neck | 麻煩的事 | generally speaking | 一般來說 |
| reduce | v. 減少 | unit | n. 單位 |
| estimation | n. 估計 | spot | v. 看到 |
| vast | adj. 廣大的 | embarrassed | adj. 尷尬的 |

# Vegetarian Meal
# 素食餐點

*Allen* / 店員

*Customer* / 客人

*Jeremy* / 股東

 ## 情境對話

 MP3 38

**Customer :** I'd like to know if you have vegetarian meals **available**?

客人：我想請問貴餐廳是否提供素食餐點？

**Allen :** We have **meatless** meals available all day long.

艾倫：我們整日提供無肉餐點。

**Customer :** Not only meat, but also dairy products and eggs. Do you have egg-free meals and dairy **alternatives**?

客人：不只是肉而已，還包括奶類製品及雞蛋。你們有無蛋餐點和其他奶類可以選擇嗎？

**Allen :** Hold on please, I'll ask about that right now.

**Jeremy :** Allen, how many times do I have to tell you that we can **customize** a vegan meal?

**Allen :** But do we have an egg-free meal? I don't think so.

**Jeremy :** Yes, we do. Cathy uses flax seed for an egg **substitute**.

**Allen :** Wow, I didn't know that.

**Allen :** Hi, we do have egg-free meals, and we can also customize your food under your special requests. If you **prefer** any kind of vegan milk, please let us know.

**Customer :** You saved the day!

艾倫：請稍等，我立刻幫您確認。

傑瑞米：艾倫，我要講幾次，你才會記住我們可以客製素食餐點？

艾倫：但是我們也提供無蛋餐點嗎？我以為沒有。

傑瑞米：有，凱西用亞麻子代替雞蛋。

艾倫：哇，這我可不知道。

艾倫：您好，我們的確有無蛋餐點，我們還可以依據您的需求提供客製化餐點。若您有偏好的植物奶，請讓我們知道。

客人：你們真是太棒了！

 **哪裡有問題**

客人致電詢問店內是否提供素食餐點，艾倫在向傑瑞米確認後，回答可以客製化客人想要的餐點。素食是個嚴肅的議題，而這在世界各大城市更是越來越普遍的現象。以洛杉磯為例，因為人們追求纖細的身材，越來越多餐館提供全素餐點。素食從預備食材到烹調，每個步驟都必須完全與葷食隔離。因此能否恰當的烹煮素食，對餐廳是嚴肅的課題。

# 餐飲補充包

In the western diet, meat is the star of almost every main courses. Having meat means having a meal, this has been a **tradition throughout** ages. However, this tradition has been **twisted** strongly in **modern** society. Unlike Asians that **forbid** meat-eating **based on** their **belief**, the Westerners give up meat **for the sake of civilized** diseases and shape-**maintenance**.

There are two kinds of vegetarians in the west: one is the vegetarian that **consumes** egg and dairy products, the other is vegan that **forfeits** all animal-related ingredients. In western cuisine, eggs, butter and cheese are the center of many dishes. Hence, a restaurant that uses vegan butter, milk alternatives and egg substitutes is a rare thing.

Since the Westerners don't have the **habit** of consuming fake meat, vegetarians eat only vegetables **literally**. Vegetarianism and veganism are serious subjects in many regions.

# 中譯

西方國家的飲食中，肉類是主菜的代表。有肉就有吃飯的感覺，這是幾世紀以來沿襲的傳統，然而這樣的傳統卻在近代有了巨大的改變。不同於亞洲人因宗教緣故茹素，西方人因各樣文明病、身材因素等，越來越多人不再吃肉。

西方的素食分為兩類，一是食用蛋奶素的茹素者，另一種是完全禁絕動物類製品的素食者。在西方料理中，雞蛋、奶油和起司等幾乎是料理的靈魂，因此若是一家餐廳能使用素食奶油、植物奶、雞蛋替代品等進行料理，對客人來說是很罕見的。

因為西方人沒有吃素肉的習慣，因此茹素者確實是以吃蔬菜為主，而這在許多地區是被嚴肅對待的問題。

# 字彙和慣用語一覽表

| | | | |
|---|---|---|---|
| available | adj. 可用的 | meatless | adj. 無肉的 |
| alternative | n. 選擇 | customize | v. 客製 |
| substitute | n. 替代品 | prefer | v. 偏好 |
| tradition | n. 傳統 | throughout | adj. 整個的 |
| twist | v. 扭曲 | modern | adj. 現代的 |
| forbid | v. 禁止 | base on | 以…為基礎 |
| belief | n. 信仰 | for the sake of | 為了…的緣故 |
| civilized | adj. 文明的 | maintenance | n. 維持 |
| consume | v. 消耗 | forfeit | v. 放棄 |
| habit | n. 習慣 | literally | 按照字面 |

# Unit 3.4

## Pet-friendly
## 攜帶寵物

 Allen / 店員　 Customer / 客人　 Jeremy / 股東

 **情境對話**

**Customer :** Hello, I'd like to know if it's possible to bring my pet with me to your restaurant?

客人：嗨，我想請問是否有可能帶寵物一同前去用餐呢？

**Allen :** What kind of animal do you have, if I may ask?

艾倫：我能請問是什麼樣的寵物嗎？

**Customer :** Two dogs and an **owl**.

客人：兩隻狗和一隻貓頭鷹。

**Allen :** I will have to ask my **supervisor**. I will get back to you **ASAP**.

艾倫：我必須問問老闆。我會盡快回覆您。

192

**Allen :** Jeremy, someone just called to check if she can dine with her two doggies and an owl.

艾倫：傑瑞米，剛剛有人打電話來，想問是否能帶她的兩隻狗和貓頭鷹一起來用餐。

**Jeremy :** Ha-ha! I don't think so. It's very **disturbing** for other diners. No way!

傑瑞米：哈！我可不同意，這會嚴重干擾其他客人，不行！

**Allen :** What about just the dogs? Can they come along?

艾倫：如果只帶狗呢？狗能進來嗎？

**Jeremy :** No! It is not only a matter of **tranquility**, but also a matter of **hygiene**.

傑瑞米：不行！這不僅是妨害安寧的問題，更有衛生上的疑慮。

**Allen : Alrighty**. I think she won't be happy about the answer.

艾倫：好吧，我想她不會喜歡我的答案。

**Allen :** I'm sorry, but I'm afraid that our restaurant can't **provide** an environment for you and your pets.

艾倫：我很抱歉，但我怕我們餐廳不適合您和您的寵物。

**Customer :** That's **depressing**!

客人：唉呀！真令人失望！

193

# 哪裡有問題

在亞洲，寵物友善餐廳是個漸漸興起的潮流，甚至有許多店家以「店狗」、「貓店長」為賣點，帶起不小的人氣，也有飼主們帶著寵物在這類餐廳進行聚會。西方國家相對而言較沒有如此這般對寵物友善的用餐環境，因為寵物毛髮、流行病及個人觀感等問題，大多數餐廳是不能攜帶寵物的。若遇顧客詢問，餐廳方需有智慧的說明原因，才不致引起寵物主人的不愉快。

# 餐飲補充包

Whether the restaurant accepts pets depends not only on the **type** of the restaurant, but also on the feeling of its owner. Since many family-style diners and coffee shops are more casual, not official dining places, seeing customers dining with their cats and dogs are more common. Even the owners may keep their pets outside their restaurants. However, in the places that **expect** tips, one can **hardly** see any animals in there.

**Regarding** the **unpredictable** behavior and **potential** diseases of the animals, these can be a big disturbance for other diners. **As a consequence**, in most of the **high-ends** restaurants, pets are forbidden in order to avoid any possible arguments. Even **tying** the pets outside the restaurant should be permitted by the owner of the restaurant.

Although eating out is not fun for the pets, Westerners are very **fond of** their animals. If the owner of the restaurant allows the pets to enter the store, he is usually not only friendly, but might even be warm enough to provide food and water for them!

# 中譯

一家餐廳是否接受動物進入，除了依據餐廳的性質進行考量外，也依據店主的脾氣決定。大部分家庭式的餐館和咖啡館，算是較為隨興、非正式的用餐場所，較常看到客人帶著貓狗一同用餐，甚至店主自己也會在店外養寵物。但在需付小費的餐廳，幾乎是沒見過允許寵物入內的。

考慮到寵物不一定都會乖乖待在主人身邊，若是引起其他客人的困擾就麻煩了，另外也有疾病等衛生上的考量，因此在價位較高的餐廳，寵物都是謝絕入內的。儘管只是將寵物綁在店門外，最好也要在取得店家同意的情況下進行。

雖說大環境下，在外用餐對寵物而言相對不友善，但是西方社會人們都非常喜愛動物，因此只要在店主允許寵物的場所，往往店主不僅對寵物友善，甚至還會拿食物和水給牠們呢！

# 字彙和慣用語一覽表

| | | | |
|---|---|---|---|
| owl | n. 貓頭鷹 | supervisor | n. 監督 |
| ASAP | =as soon as possible | disturb | v. 打擾 |
| tranquility | n. 安寧 | hygiene | n. 衛生 |
| alrighty | =alright | provide | v. 提供 |
| depressing | adj. 令人憂鬱的 | type | n. 類型 |
| spot | n. 地方 | expect | v. 期待 |
| hardly | adv. 幾乎不 | regarding | 關於 |
| unpredictable | adj. 不可預期的 | potential | adj. 可能的 |
| as a consequence | 結果 | high-ends | 高檔的 |
| tie | v. 繫 | be fond of | 喜歡 |

# Kid-friendly
# 親子用餐

 Allen / 店員　 Customer / 客人　Jeremy / 股東

##  情境對話

 MP3 40

**Customer :** Afternoon. I'd like to ask if there is a baby chair in your restaurant?

客人：下午好，我想請問貴餐廳是否提供嬰兒椅呢？

**Allen :** I'm afraid that we only have a children's chair, ma'am.

艾倫：我想我們僅提供兒童椅，女士。

**Customer :** Could you make sure? It's very important for us.

客人：你可以確認一下嗎？這對我們來說很重要。

**Allen :** Jeremy, a customer is asking if we have a baby chair.

艾倫：傑瑞米，有客人詢問我們是否提供嬰兒椅。

**Jeremy :** That must be an **infant**. We do not accept kids under 3.

**Allen :** That's bad news. But why?

**Jeremy :** It's dangerous to have infants around. They may get **burned** by soup, they may fall, and **worst of all**, they may cry and scream! We don't want any part of these troubles.

**Allen : Fair enough**. It's safer for kids to stay home after all.

**Allen :** Sorry, we do not accept kids under 3 years old. I'm terribly sorry, ma'am.

**Customer :** That's Okay. I understand. Thank you though.

傑瑞米：一定是還在襁褓中的孩子，我們不接受三歲以下的兒童。

艾倫：真是壞消息，但是為什麼呢？

傑瑞米：有嬰兒在附近很危險，他們可能被湯燙到、跌下椅子，更糟的是，他們會哭和尖叫！我們可不想有這些麻煩事發生。

艾倫：好吧，孩子們還是待在家裡比較安全。

艾倫：抱歉，我們不接受三歲以下的小孩。我真的很抱歉，女士。

客人：沒關係，我了解。還是謝謝你。

# 哪裡有問題

當客人帶著孩子上餐廳時,餐廳服務人員的職責就不只是上餐而已。

嬰兒、孩童有各自專用的座椅,當有需要時,往往需要將一般椅子撤走並換上專用座椅,這需要外場人員的快速應變,才不會讓客人久候。

另外,孩童需使用專用的餐具,通常是摔不破的類型,並遠離玻璃製品。

文中艾倫工作的餐廳不接待三歲以下的孩子,這能直接地避免服務不周或兒童受傷的問題。

# 餐飲補充包

Are kids **supposed to** be allowed in a restaurant? What if they cry and get loud, and **annoy** other customers? Or, if the kids get hurt **accidentally**, who is **responsible for** it? Because of these **controversial subjects**, more and more restaurants forbid not only pets, but also young kids.

Usually, this **restriction** is applied to high-end restaurants. **Contrary to** these ones, there are restaurants that **feature** on being kids-friendly. In Asia, there is an **increasing** number of these kids-friendly restaurants. Just like McDonald's, these places **provide** fun areas for kids, as well as **professional** services.

Before dining or working in these places, it is important to make **clear** which kind of restaurant one is going to be at. Different services are asked for different needs; this is an **essential concept** for people that work in the food **industry**.

**中譯**

餐廳是否該接待孩童？若是孩童哭鬧，造成其他顧客的不便，或是孩童不小心受傷，責任該由誰來負？因為茲事體大，越來越多的餐廳除了標榜禁止寵物外，也不准太過年幼的孩童入場。

通常，在較高價位的餐廳較會有此限制。而與這種餐廳相反的，是以親子餐廳為號召的用餐場所。在亞洲，有越來越多歡迎父母帶學齡前子女前往用餐的親子餐廳，就像麥當勞一樣，這些地方設有供孩子玩耍的空間，也有針對孩子的專業服務。

在前往餐廳用餐或工作前，搞清楚餐廳的型態是相當重要的。針對不同需求，餐廳員工提供的服務也不同，這是餐飲業人員應有的重要觀念。

**字彙和慣用語一覽表**

| | | | |
|---|---|---|---|
| infant | n. 嬰兒 | burn | v. 燙傷 |
| worst of all | 最糟的是 | fair enough | 好啦；是喔 |
| be supposed to | 應該要 | annoy | v. 纏人 |
| accidently | adv. 意外地 | responsible for | 為…負責 |
| controversial | adj. 爭議性的 | subject | n. 主題 |
| restriction | n. 限制 | contrary to | 與…相反 |
| feature | v. 以…為特色 | increasing | adj. 增加中的 |
| provide | v. 提供 | professional | adj. 職業的 |
| clear | adj. 明白的 | essential | adj. 必要的 |
| concept | n. 概念 | industry | n. 產業 |

# Birthday Surprise Party
# 生日驚喜派對

Allen / 店員

Customer / 客人

Jeremy / 股東

 **情境對話**

**Customer :** Hello, is this Classic American?

**Allen :** Yes, ma'am. What can I do for you?

**Customer :** I'm thinking of **throwing a** surprise birthday **party** for my daughter's sixteenth birthday. Is it possible for us to hold the party in your restaurant? There will be about 20 people, and I hope to arrange all the tables together, in a circle.

客人：嗨，這裡是經典小美式嗎？

艾倫：是的，有甚麼能為您服務的嗎？

客人：我在想要替我女兒舉辦一個 16 歲的驚喜生日派對。有可能在你們餐廳裡舉辦嗎？大約會有 20 人左右，我希望大家能聚在一起為成一圈。

**Alen :** Sounds fun! I just have to make sure before I give you a **solid** answer, so if I may, I'll get back to you in just a few moments.

艾倫：聽起來很有趣！在給您確實答案前，我要先做確認？，所以如果可以的話，我再過一會兒就能回覆你了。

**Allen :** Jeremy, some woman said that she'd like to throw a birthday party in our place. 20 people all **at once** and they want to sit together.

艾倫：傑瑞米,有幾個女人説她們想要在我們這裡辦個生日派對。一次二十人，然後他們想要坐在一起。

**Jeremy :** What a mess…it's gonna be crazy that day.

傑瑞米：真糟糕透了…那天將會很瘋狂。

**Allen :** I can see that. Should I accept it?

艾倫：我能想像那情況。我該接受這要求嗎？

**Jeremy :** What about asking her if she wants **catering**? We can cater her party instead.

傑瑞米：要嘛問她是否需要外燴服務？取而代之的是我們可以承辦他的聚會。

**Allen :** **Genius** idea!

艾倫：超棒的想法！

 # 哪裡有問題

當客人告知將在餐廳裡舉行特殊活動的聚會時，餐廳老闆常會陷入兩難的抉擇。

一方面，這樣來客數穩定，就能期待當天營業額提升；另一方面，客人點餐的數量不一定，且客人待在餐廳的時間較久，難以有新客人流動。還有一面的考量是，舉行慶祝活動的客人可能太過吵雜，影響其他顧客的觀感。

文中傑瑞米提議進行外燴服務，若是餐廳人手充足，這會是較為恰當的決定。

# 餐飲補充包

A big group of people is a **nerve-wracking** thing for the restaurant **staff**. People all coming at once **requires** more attention from the staff, and if each one of them needs special service, it would just be a **hot mess**.

Not only that, with the tickets getting to the kitchen **altogether**, it results in **chaos** and the **delay** of meal serving. If there is a group reservation, servers must be **on their toes**. It is better to take the orders **separately**, instead of taking them all at once. In bigger, chain restaurants, it is common that there is a birthday special for the person. It could be a discount or free dessert. However, in smaller, family-style restaurants, whether the **bonus** is given out **totally** relies on the owner's decision.

As a server, one should know to **read the air**, and talk to the owner about it when one sees **fit**. Sometimes a little gift will **put out** a bigger and better **image** of the restaurant, and that is what brings back the customers.

# 中譯

人數多的預約團體，對餐廳工作人員來說是令人緊張的一件事。同時間湧入許多人，不僅在招呼上需要反應更靈敏，若是客人有特別需要，往往應付起來會有點手忙腳亂。

另一方面，同一時間湧入的點單會造成廚房的混亂，也會延遲上餐，因此若遇團體預約的狀況，外場人員特別須注意，最好讓客人分別點餐，而非在同一時段點所有人的餐。另外，較大型的連鎖餐廳常會有生日壽星優惠，可能是打折或贈送甜點等，但在較小的家庭式餐廳，是否要有優惠服務，就考慮店主的智慧了。

身為店員，可以隨機應變，適時的提醒老闆，也許可以送些小禮，讓客人留下好印象，進而造成回流。

# 字彙和慣用語一覽表

| | | | |
|---|---|---|---|
| throw a party | 開派對 | solid | adj. 確定的 |
| at once | 一次 | catering | n. 外燴 |
| genius | adj. 天才的 | nerve-wracking | adj. 緊張的 |
| staff | n. 工作人員 | require | v. 要求 |
| hot mess | 一團糟 | altogether | adv. 一起 |
| chaos | n. 混亂 | delay | n. 延遲 |
| on sb's toes | 待命 | separately | adv. 分開地 |
| bonus | n. 紅利 | totally | adv. 總共地 |
| read the air | 察言觀色 | fit | adj. 適合的 |
| put out | 發放 | image | n. 形象 |

# Unit 4.1 Food Concerns
## 對料理細節有疑慮

 Allen / 店員　　 Customer / 客人　　 Jeremy / 股東

 情境對話　　 MP3 42

**Customer :** Excuse me? Are there any dairy products in my potato pancakes?

客人：不好意思，請問我的馬鈴薯餅裡有奶製品嗎？

**Allen :** I'm not sure sir. I don't think so.

艾倫：先生，我不太確定，應該沒有吧。

**Customer :** You're not sure? I'm **allergic** to dairy! Do you want to be responsible for the consequences of **uncertain** ingredients in your dish?

客人：你不確定？我對奶製品過敏！你想對食物裡不確定的原料造成的後果負責嗎？

210

**Allen :** Sorry sir, I'll get the **details** right now. (In the kitchen)

艾倫：抱歉，我立刻去確認。（在廚房）

**Cathy :** There's milk in the pancake.

凱西：馬鈴薯餅裡有牛奶。

**Allen : Geez**! That old guy is gonna be so **pissed**!

艾倫：我的天！那位老傢伙一定很生氣。

**Jeremy :** It is serious, **dude**. If we get any customer sick with **false** information, it's our problem! Ask before you answer any question again like that, you hear me?

傑瑞米：這很嚴重，老兄。如果我們的客人因為錯誤的訊息生病了，那可是我們的錯。之後再有像這樣的問題，先問清楚再回答，懂了嗎？

**Allen :** Alright. I think that guy needs some different pancakes then.

艾倫：好的。我想那位客人需要一些不同的煎餅。

**Allen :** Sir, here are your non-dairy potato pancakes.

艾倫：先生，這是您的無奶馬鈴薯餅。

**Customer :** That's better. Watch out next time, will ya? For God's sake!

客人：這樣好多了。下次注意點好嗎？看在老天的份上！

 # 哪裡有問題

就像素餐也分蛋奶素、奶素等等一樣，每個人對食物的要求都不一樣。在美國，對奶、蛋、麩質（麥子）過敏的人尤其不在少數。與華人不同的是，歐美較沒有因信仰而有食品禁忌，通常都是因過敏現象嚴重的緣故。因此，為避免造成顧客身體不適，侍者應了解餐廳中每道料理的原料。對話中的艾倫就差點因不求甚解的態度，害老人家生病了。

# 餐飲補充包

Being certain and clear about every dish on the menu is the responsibility of any server. By giving out exact and **precise** answers, a server **showcases** that he/she is professional. Not only this, it is also very important that the diners know what they are receiving. Food allergy is a common **issue** today.

As a consequence, **gluten**-free meals and **lactose**-free meals are usually much **appreciated**. Kosher diets and vegetarian meal should also be taken into concern, **just to name a few**. If these special meals are not **marked out** on the menu, the server should **be capable of** answering the question and assure that their diners are not getting anything unexpected.

To prepare oneself for any possible questions and to **achieve** the best results, it is best to taste all the dishes on the menu. If that is not easy to do, at least one can ask the cooks before serving. Do not take it lightly. Any **vague** answer can result in a serious problem, even a **lawsuit**.

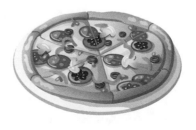

# 中譯

對菜單上的每道菜瞭若指掌是每位侍者應盡的義務，準確且精準的應答展現侍者的專業。不只如此，讓顧客知道他們將吃到什麼也很重要。在今日的社會，食品過敏是很普遍的狀況。

為此，餐廳若提供無麩質餐、無奶餐是很貼心的舉動，而猶太飲食和素食等等也需要列入考量。若是菜單上沒有標示這些餐點，侍者應該要能對來客問題應答如流，並確保他們的座上賓不會收到任何預期外的食物。

為了能給每個問題提供答覆，並為了賓主盡歡，侍者最好能親自品嘗菜單上的每道菜。若是無法一一品嘗，至少也要在送餐前先行詢問。不要過度隨興。任何模糊的資訊都可能造成嚴重的後果，甚至引來司法訴訟。

# 字彙和慣用語一覽表

| | | | |
|---|---|---|---|
| allergic | adj. 過敏的 | uncertain | adj. 不確定的 |
| detail | n. 細節 | geez | 天哪 |
| pissed | adj. 惱怒的 | false | adj. 錯誤的 |
| dude | 老兄、小子 | showcase | v. 展現 |
| precise | adj. 精確的 | gluten | n. 麩質 |
| issue | n. 問題 | appreciated | adj. 受感謝的 |
| lactose | n. 乳糖 | mark out | 標示 |
| just to name a few | 僅列一二 | achieve | v. 做到 |
| be capable of | 能夠… | lawsuit | n. 官司 |
| vague | adj. 模糊的 | | |

# Changing Orders
## 更換餐點

 Allen /店員　 Customer /客人　 Jeremy /股東

 **情境對話**

**Customer :** Excuse me, is my banana split ready yet?

客人：不好意思，請問我的香蕉船做好了嗎？

**Allen :** Sorry, Ma'am, it'll be right up.

艾倫：抱歉，女士，馬上就好了。

**Customer :** Oh, actually, I'm wondering if I could change it to strawberry French toast instead?

客人：噢，其實我在想，是不是有可能換成草莓法式吐司呢？

**Allen :** Ma'am, I'm afraid that your banana split is already being made, and we **are unable to**…

艾倫：女士，我怕香蕉船已經在做了，我們沒辦法…

**Jeremy :** (whisper) Allen! Stop it!

**Allen :** Sir?

**Jeremy :** Don't you **dare turn down** our customer like that! If they want to change their order, let them! We provide what they want, that's our job!

**Allen :** Then what about the banana split? I think Cathy may have already made it.

**Jeremy :** That's not a problem. We must do our best to **satisfy** the customers, so you've got to say yes instead of no.

**Allen :** Got it. (To the customer.) Sure, your strawberry French toast will be ready in a few minutes.

**Customer :** **Fantastic**! Can't wait.

傑瑞米：（小聲地）艾倫！噓！

艾倫：啊？

傑瑞米：不准你那樣拒絕客人！如果他們想換，就讓他們換。我們負責提供客人想要的餐點，這是我們的工作。

艾倫：那香蕉船怎麼辦？我想凱西可能已經做好了。

傑瑞米：那不成問題。我們必須盡力滿足客人，所以要你向他們說「是」，而非「不」。

艾倫：我懂了。（向客人說）沒問題，您的草莓法式吐司馬上來。

客人：太棒了！我等不及了！

# 哪裡有問題

每間餐廳雖然依店主脾氣不同，不一定會讓顧客這樣半途換餐點。不過，一般來說稍有規模的餐廳，通常都不介意讓客人點他們真正想吃的料理，就算先點的餐已經快做好了也一樣。侍者遇到這種狀況時，通常左右為難，這時最好先詢問廚房或老闆，確定可以換餐再向客人確認。服務生的職責就是做好溝通的工作，千萬不要自作主張下決定喔。

# 餐飲補充包

Although it is not **frequent**, sometimes we do **encounter** changing minds **in terms of** order taking. Under these **conditions**, it is not very wise to turn down a customer's **request** immediately. Instead, a server's job is to **fulfill** the diners' needs and to make them come again. In order to achieve that, the former order, even if it has already been taken care of can be **switched** to another **option** under customer's request, a server makes sure that the answer is **affirmative**.

This is not only being considerate, but also giving out an **assuring** impression that all their needs would be met in this environment. However, it can be a pain in the neck when this situation takes place too often, especially during **rush** hours. Under these **circumstances**, it is better to **convince** the customer to **stick to** the original order.

## 中譯

雖然這種狀況並不常見，但有時的確會碰到中途改變心意的客人。在這類狀況下，斷然拒絕客人不太明智。相反的，侍者的工作是滿足顧客的要求，並讓他們再度光顧。為了達到這個目標，就算先前的點單已經在製作中，當客人要求換餐點時，侍者也應盡可能讓他們如意。

這不僅是貼心的舉動，更是讓客人對餐廳留下滿意的好印象。然而，若這種情形太頻繁，可能就很令人頭痛，特別是用餐尖峰時段。這種狀況下，最好勸顧客不要改點單比較好。

# 字彙和慣用語一覽表

| be unable to | 不能夠… | dare | v. 敢 |
|---|---|---|---|
| turn down | 拒絕 | satisfy | v. 使滿意 |
| fantastic | adj. 奇妙的 | frequent | adj. 頻繁的 |
| encounter | v. 遭遇 | in terms of | 就…而言 |
| condition | n. 狀況 | request | v. 請求 |
| fulfill | v. 落實 | switch | v. 替換 |
| option | n. 選項 | affirmative | adj. 肯定的 |
| assuring | adj. 保障的 | rush | n. 匆促 |
| circumstance | n. 狀況；環境 | convince | v. 説服 |
| stick to | 堅持 | | |

# Running out of food
# 食材用完了

*Allen* / 店員　　*Cathy* / 廚師　　*Jeremy* / 股東

 **情境對話**

**Allen :** One meatloaf, one onion soup and one chicken **club** sandwich.

艾倫：一個肉派、一個洋蔥湯和一個雞肉總匯三明治。

**Cathy :** There's no more meatloaf. The one you took out was the last order. Told you when you came in earlier, remember?

凱西：沒有肉派囉，剛剛你拿出去的是最後一份。你剛進來時我告訴你啦，記得嗎？

**Allen :** What? What **am I supposed to** do now?

艾倫：什麼？我現在怎麼辦？

**Jeremy :** What **the hell** is going on? Why are you **yelling**?

傑瑞米：發生什麼事了？你們為什麼大吼大叫？

222

**Allen :** I just had an order of meatloaf, but I wasn't paying attention when Cathy told me that we were **out of** meatloaf.

艾倫：剛剛有人點肉派，但凱西告訴我肉派賣完時，我沒注意聽。

**Jeremy :** You'll have to ask the customer to change.

傑瑞米：你去請客人換餐點吧。

**Allen :** This is **awkward**.

艾倫：好彆扭阿。

**Allen :** I'm sorry, but the meatloaf is sold out.

艾倫：我很抱歉，但是肉派賣完了。

**Customer : What a shame**! I came for meatloaf!

客人：好可惜，我就是為了肉派來的。

**Allen :** I'm really sorry. Our **cottage** pie is good too! Would you…

艾倫：我真的很抱歉。我們的農舍派也很棒，您要不要…

**Customer :** No, I'm good. I'll come next time. (Walks out of the restaurant.)

客人：不了，謝謝。我下次再來。（走出餐廳）

**Allen :** Oh, **that sucks**.

艾倫：噢，感覺真壞。

# 哪裡有問題

對話中，艾倫沒注意到肉派已經沒有了，造成點餐後又
向客人取消。這種情況想也知道很尷尬，畢竟造成來客
的失望，心裡多少不舒坦。要避免這狀況，當然不是三
不五時到廚房巡視，只要在廚師告知的時候多留心就可
以了。廚師和服務生的溝通很重要，若是廚師出餐時剛
好將食材用完，卻忘了告訴外場服務生，可能就會造成
不愉快。

# 餐飲補充包

It is very important that a server **is aware of** the situation in the kitchen. Their information should be **up-to-date**, in order to take **proper** orders and give out **recommendations**. For instance, when a customer asks for ordering **advice**, the server had better make sure that his or her recommendations are available on that day.

**Otherwise**, not only might the customer be disappointed, but it also shows a **lack of** training in the restaurant team. As for kitchen staff, every single bit of information should be **passed out**. If a certain ingredient or a dish is sold out, the whole team should be **informed**. It is always a shame to take an order in and change it against the customer's will.

This usually happens during rush hours, like an hour and half into dinner service. The staff can be so **backed up** that they forget about **communication**.

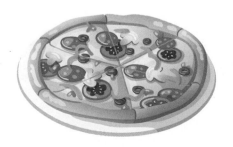

**中譯**

掌握廚房的狀況對侍者來說相當重要，他們必須得知每項資訊，才能合適的點餐並推薦菜餚。舉例來說，當一位客人尋求點餐建議時，侍者應確認他所推薦的菜色當天有供應。

否則不僅客人會很失望，連帶顯示餐廳團隊的訓練不足。至於廚房工作人員，則應將每件細節通知所有團隊成員。若是某項食材或菜餚賣完了，整個團隊都應該被告知。若是在點了餐之後，又違背顧客的意願更換餐點，這實在很可惜。

在用餐尖峰時段，比如用餐開始一個半小時後，這事比較常發生；有時因為太忙，團隊成員會忘記彼此溝通。

# 字彙和慣用語一覽表

| | | | |
|---|---|---|---|
| club | n. 俱樂部 | be supposed to | 應該 |
| the hell | 搞什麼；見鬼 | yell | v. 大吼 |
| out of | …用完了 | awkward | adj. 笨拙的 |
| what a shame | 很可惜 | cottage | n. 農舍 |
| sth. sucks | 某事很糟糕 | be aware of | 意識到 |
| up-to-date | adj. 最新的 | proper | adj. 合宜的 |
| recommendation | n. 推薦 | advise | v. 建議 |
| otherwise | adv. 否則 | lack of | 缺乏 |
| pass out | 送出 | informed | adj. 被通知的 |
| be backed up | 很忙碌 | communication | n. 溝通 |

# Breaking Tableware
# 打破餐具

 Allen /店員　　 Customer /客人　　 Jeremy /股東

 **情境對話**

A kid drops a glass and the juice **spills**.

一個孩子將杯子摔到地上，果汁灑了出來。

**Customer：**Oh my **gosh**! Look what you did!

客人：天哪！看看你做了什麼好事！

**Allen：**That's Okay. I'll take care of it.

艾倫：沒關係，我來處理。

Allen collects all the broken glasses and **wipes** up the liquid. Then he returns to the kitchen, where he **encounters** Jeremy.

艾倫撿起杯子碎片並擦乾果汁，接著回到廚房，那兒他遇到傑瑞米。

**Jeremy :** Refill another glass of juice for them.

**Allen :** Why? They only paid for one glass of juice.

**Jeremy :** Doesn't matter. They did pay for one glass, but if we show our **generosity**, they will be **impressed**.

Allen takes a new glass and starts **pouring** the juice.

**Jeremy :** They must feel terribly sorry right now. Don't forget to smile and tell them everything's fine.

**Allen :** Here's your juice. (To the kid.) Be careful, do not let it **slip** from your hand again, okay?

**Kid :** I won't. Thank you.

傑瑞米：盛一杯新的果汁給他們。

艾倫：為什麼？他們只付了一杯果汁的錢。

傑瑞米：沒關係。他們的確只付了一杯的錢，但若是我們顯得慷慨，他們會對我們印象深刻。

艾倫拿了新的杯子並開始倒入果汁。

傑瑞米：他們現在一定覺得很抱歉。別忘了笑著告訴他們一切都很好。

艾倫：你的果汁。（對著孩子說）小心喔，別再讓杯子從你手中滑掉了，好嗎？

孩子：我不會的，謝謝你。

**哪裡有問題**

餐廳有客人打破餐具、孩子弄翻盤子等，並不是太少見的事，問題是這時候業主是要自行負擔並重新做一盤食物呢，還是留給客人空盤子？作為侍者，這時候當然以頂頭上司的意見為主。一般來說，為了顯得友善、慷慨，店主不一定會送上免費餐點，但至少會有小點心，安撫客人受驚的心情。根據店主反應的不同，會決定客人的回流率。

# 餐飲補充包

The **tableware** is usually made of glass in most of the restaurants. It is not **rare** that the customers break a plate or two. However, in this situation, a server should **deal with** it immediately. Make sure all the **fragments** are picked up, and clean up the **mess** around the area.

Sometimes, in order to avoid **further** damage (no matter who), seats changes are necessary. If the owners are thoughtful, they might prepare plastic tableware for certain customers. But it is not very common. Ask the owner about it, and give out the info **simultaneously**. Some people do appreciate the consideration of plastic tableware, especially parents with kids.

If an accident **occurs**, it **depends on** the floor manager or the owner to decide if the customer gets a new plate of food. Although it sure is a kind move, it should be left for the **authority figure** to make decisions. **All in all**, make sure that you as a server don't break anything yourself. Otherwise, it's gonna be a problem.

# 中譯

在大多數餐廳，餐具多是玻璃製的，客人打破一兩個盤子並非罕見的事。然而，在這種情況下，侍者應該立即處理，確保所有玻璃碎片都被清理乾淨、並處理該區的髒污。

有時候為了避免造成其他損害（不論是對誰而言），會需要幫客人換位子。如果店主夠體貼，他們會為特定顧客準備塑膠餐具，不過這並不常見。侍者應先行詢問店主，並主動告知顧客。有的人真的會感激有塑膠餐具，特別是對那些有孩子的父母。

若是意外發生，須由店經理或店東決定是否要為客人重做餐點。雖然這個舉動很體貼，但還是讓有權的人來決定較佳。總之，打破東西的人不要是侍者自己就好，不然，後果可能很麻煩。

# 字彙和慣用語一覽表

| | | | |
|---|---|---|---|
| spill | v. 潑灑 | gosh | 天呀 |
| wipe | v. 擦拭 | encounter | v. 遭遇 |
| generosity | n. 慷慨 | impressed | adj. 印象深刻的 |
| pour | v. 倒 | slip | v. 滑 |
| tableware | n. 餐具 | rare | adj. 罕見的 |
| deal with | 處理 | fragment | n. 碎片 |
| mess | n. 髒亂 | further | adv. 進一步 |
| simultaneously | adv. 自發地 | occur | v. 發生 |
| depend on | 取決於 | authority | n. 權柄 |
| figure | n. 人物 | all in all | 總而言之 |

# Unit 4.5 Wrong Table 上錯桌

*Allen* / 店員

*Customer* / 客人

*Jeremy* / 股東

 情境對話

**Customer :** Excuse me, we didn't order pasta.

顧客：不好意思，我們沒有點義大利麵。

**Allen :** Oh, really? I saw it on your ticket.

艾倫：哦，真的嗎？但我在你們的點單上有看到。

**Customer :** We really didn't order it. We have **sliders**, pizza, and fried **squid**, but no pasta.

顧客：我們真的沒點。我們點了迷你漢堡、披薩和炸墨魚，但沒有點義大利麵。

**Allen :** I'm very sorry. I'll check with the kitchen again.

艾倫：我很抱歉。我會跟廚房確認。

Jeremy **catches** Allen **on the way** back to the kitchen.

**Jeremy :** The food went to the wrong table?

**Allen :** Yeah, they said they didn't order pasta.

**Jeremy :** It didn't show on the ticket?

**Allen :** I thought it was theirs. Maybe I made a mistake. I'll have to double check.

**Jeremy :** That plate can't go to another table. They'll have to make a new one.

**Allen :** But they haven't touched the food.

**Jeremy :** How do you know? It has sat on their table for 5 minutes. Just make a new one, and make sure this time bring it to the **assigned** table!

傑瑞米半途攔下艾倫。

傑瑞米：食物送錯桌？

艾倫：對，他們說他們沒點義大利麵。

傑瑞米：你是沒看清楚點單嗎？

艾倫：我以為是他們的，可能是我搞錯了。我會確認看看。

傑瑞米：這盤不能送去別桌，必須重作。

艾倫：但他們根本沒動阿。

傑瑞米：你又知道了？這都放在他們桌上五分鐘了！做新的一盤就是，然後確定這次送到正確的桌號去！

# 哪裡有問題

餐飲業有時候會遇到的狀況，就是餐點送錯桌。如果只是桌號搞錯，雖然有點尷尬，道歉一下送到正確的桌去也就解決了；但若是服務生點錯餐點，可能就造成食材浪費了。對話裡無人認領的義大利麵，就是這類羅生門案的例子。既然沒有人點餐，也不能就這麼放著，幸運的話當成員工餐吃了，不幸的話，老闆可能會扣薪呢！

# 餐飲補充包

In the food industry, servers are the **bridge** between diners and cooks. They not only serve food, but also serve it to the right **destination**. Usually, in a restaurant, the tables are **numbered**. Each table gets its own server.

After the orders are taken, the server needs to **deliver** the food to the right table. If food goes to the wrong table, it's kind of **embarrassing**. However, it's not a real big deal **comparing to** wrong orders. Since each server is responsible for certain tables, they should be able to **memorize** the dishes being ordered. **Nevertheless**, in some **cases**, the diners will **claim** that they didn't order the food that's being served.

The best **response** to this is to **apologize** and quickly inform the kitchen for the right order. Do not **insist** on your impression or **opinion**, since that may **lead to** a bad **impression** of not only to the server but also of the whole business.

# 中譯

在餐飲業中，侍者是客人和廚師間的橋樑。他們不僅負責送餐，更將餐點送到正確的對象那裡。通常餐廳裡的桌子都有編號，每張桌子有專屬侍者。

點餐後，該侍者負責將餐點送至客人桌上。若是餐點送錯桌，那還滿尷尬的。不過，比起點單記錯，送錯桌還沒什麼。由於每位侍者都負責特定桌次，因此他們理應記得客人點了哪道菜。然而，有時候餐點上桌時，客人卻會聲稱他們並沒有點該道菜。

這時候最好的辦法就是道歉，並盡速將正確的餐點告知廚房。不要對自己的印象或意見緊咬不放，不然不只可能讓顧客對你的印象變差，連帶對餐廳都會大扣分。

# 字彙和慣用語一覽表

| | | | |
|---|---|---|---|
| slider | n. 迷你漢堡 | squid | n. 烏賊 |
| catch sb. on the way | 半途遇上某人 | assign | v. 分配 |
| bridge | n. 橋梁 | destination | n. 目的地 |
| number | v. 編號 | deliver | v. 傳送 |
| embarrassing | adj. 令人尷尬的 | compare to | 與…比較 |
| memorize | v. 記憶 | nevertheless | adv. 雖說 |
| case | n. 案件 | claim | v. 宣稱 |
| response | n. 反應 | apologize | v. 道歉 |
| insist | v. 堅持 | opinion | n. 看法 |
| lead to | 導致 | impression | n. 印象 |

# Returned Food
# 餐點退回

Allen / 店員

Jeremy / 股東

 情境對話

MP3
47

Jeremy **spots** that Allen taking a plate of food back to the kitchen.

傑瑞米發現艾倫拿著裝滿食物的盤子回到廚房。

**Jeremy :** What's that about?

傑瑞米：那是怎麼回事？

**Allen :** Customers at Table two are complaining about the food, so I have to bring it back.

艾倫：二桌的客人對食物有微詞，所以我必須拿回來。

**Jeremy :** How did that happen?

傑瑞米：怎麼會這樣呢？

**Allen :** They said that the meat in the burger was cold and the sauce was **soupy**. The salad greens had dirt on them, and **worst of all**, they found hair in the plate.

艾倫：他們説漢堡肉是冷的，醬汁太多湯水，沙拉葉有土，最糟的是，他們在盤子裡發現頭髮。

**Jeremy :** What the hell? Tell the chef to remake everything, and find out who is responsible for all this!

傑瑞米：搞什麼啊？告訴主廚重做一份，並找出是誰闖的禍！

**Allen :** What about the customers? They seem pretty **upset**.

艾倫：那客人怎麼辦？他們看起來很生氣。

**Jeremy :** Give them free desserts as an apology. **Tag** a discount card along with it. I can't believe this is happening in my restaurant. You guys are **pissing me off**!

傑瑞米：招待他們免費甜點表達歉意，還要附上折扣卡。真不敢相信我的餐廳會出這種包！你們惹火我了！

**Allen :** Yes, sir. Right away.

艾倫：是，老闆，我馬上去。

# 哪裡有問題

通常在歐美國家的餐廳用餐，費用都會比較高，因此，若是餐點不合意，基本上都可以跟服務生反應並要求重作。常發生的情形像是出餐錯誤（點牛排拿到魚排）、食物冷掉、餐具不乾淨…等。為維護餐廳形象並安撫客人，老闆或經理通常會送上免費甜點或贈送折扣卡。若不是真的令客人非常不愉快的用餐經驗，通常不至於免費用餐。

# 餐飲補充包

Fresh food is the most **crucial** point of running a restaurant. Food being returned is a sign of serving bad food, which shows customers' **dissatisfaction**. Cold dishes, aside from salads and certain soups, are a sign of low standards in the kitchen and a **lack** of care. Usually, food should be made **by order**, fresh and new.

Made-ahead food is usually unacceptable, not to mention **reheated** (or even worse, microwaved) dishes. Underdone/ overdone meat is another reason of food being returned. **Undercooked** meat could lead to **contamination** and diseases, whereas **overcooked** meat can be tough and **rubbery**. For instance, undercooked scallops are **chewy** and bland.

Apart from these reasons, uncleaned ingredients and dirty **tableware** can also give diners bad **impressions**. Since a restaurant business is based on repeat customers, the owners will do every effort to maintain and **improve** the food as well as the dining **environment**.

# 中譯

新鮮的食材是經營餐廳的首要條件。食物被退回代表餐點美味度待加強，同時也反映客人的不滿。除了沙拉或某些湯品之外，冷掉的食物表示廚房標準低劣，食材不受重視。一般來說，食物應在收到點單之後才做，這樣才會新鮮。

把料理做好放著不是好事，更別提重新加熱（或更糟，微波過的食品）的剩菜了。烹調不夠或煮過頭的肉類是另一個食物被退回的原因。烹調不夠的肉會導致細菌汙染及疾病，煮過頭的肉則是過硬而難咬。舉例而言，烹調不足的扇貝很難咀嚼且淡而無味。

除了上述原因之外，不潔的食材和骯髒的餐具也會給客人壞印象。正因餐廳的經營在於顧客回流，因此店東總是致力維持食物水準，並改善用餐環境。

# 字彙和慣用語一覽表

| | | | |
|---|---|---|---|
| spot | v. 發現；看到 | soupy | adj. 稀的；湯汁的 |
| worst of all | 最糟的是… | upset | adj. 惱怒；沮喪 |
| tag | v. 尾隨 | piss sb. off | 惹某人生氣 |
| crucial | adj. 緊要的 | dissatisfaction | n. 不滿足 |
| lack | n. 缺乏 | by order | 根據點單／命令 |
| reheat | v. 重新加熱 | undercook | adj. 烹調不足的 |
| overcook | adj. 烹調過度的 | contamination | n. 汙染 |
| rubbery | adj. 橡膠般的 | chewy | adj. 有嚼勁的 |
| tableware | n. 餐具 | impression | n. 印象 |
| improve | v. 改進 | environment | n. 環境 |

Part

2

餐飲搶分篇

Unit

04

Customer Service 客訴處理

# Returned Food 2
# 餐點退回 2

*Allen* / 店員    *Cathy* / 廚師    *Jeremy* / 股東

 **情境對話**

MP3
48

**Cathy :** What's wrong with that **elk**?

凱西：那盤鹿肉怎麼了？

**Allen :** The customer says it is not cooked all the way through.

艾倫：客人說沒有完全煮熟。

**Cathy :** How's that possible?

凱西：怎麼可能？

**Allen :** That's what she says. Could you give it a taste?

艾倫：她的確這麼說。妳要不要吃吃看？

**Cathy :** It's medium-rare; it's good.

凱西：這是五分熟，很好吃呀。

**Allen :** Well, I suppose that she wants it well-done.

**Cathy :** If so, the elk will be **rubbery** and tough. She won't like it. I **guarantee**.

**Jeremy :** Cathy, do not **hold on to** your own **preference**. Just do as the customer asks.

**Cathy :** But…what if she tastes it and says that we don't know how to cook elk? We did it right, but it's not to her taste. That's all. It's not fair to be complained to about this.

**Jeremy :** What if you explain it to her, Allen? Make sure the customer understands the result. If she still wants a well-done elk, we can do that.

**Allen :** Right away, sir.

艾倫：我猜她想要全熟。

凱西：全熟的鹿肉很難咬、很硬的。她不會喜歡的，我保證。

傑瑞米：凱西，不要緊咬自己的意見不放，就照客人要求的去做。

凱西：但要是她吃了之後，説我們不懂料理鹿肉怎麼辦？我們煮的方法很正確，只是不合她的口味，僅此而已。要是因為這樣被抱怨，我覺得有失公道。

傑瑞米：艾倫，你何不解釋給客人聽呢？讓她了解結果，如果她還是要全熟的鹿肉，我們可以照辦。

艾倫：我立刻去。

# 哪裡有問題

有時烹調得正確且美味的餐點，仍可能被退回廚房。
其中原因不乏顧客吃不慣餐點口味，或烹調方式不合客
人期望等。在亞洲社會，因華人對肉品的認知與西方稍
有不同，因此常發生客人對肉排的熟度不滿意，而退回
餐點之情況。同樣的，在西方社會，中式餐點也常需照
當地飲食習慣做調整，才能迎合大眾的口味。

## 餐飲補充包

If the chef doesn't have proper cooking skills, **resulting in** the dish being returned, there is nothing to say. However, what to do when the food is cooked perfectly, yet the **complaints** still occur? Take the dining environment in Taiwan for example, nowadays, Italian restaurants are everywhere.

Pasta dishes and risotto are nothing **rare**. Nevertheless, most people are not **knowledgeable** about the al-dente condition of Italian dishes, which is the slightly underdone **texture** of the grains. This is for the **grains** not getting **mushy** after mixing in the sauce. Yet for **average** Asian people, this condition **equals** being "uncooked", and thusly they **criticize** the professionalism of the chef.

Since it's impossible to ask the customers to be fully **equipped with** the knowledge, if the dish is returned for the above reasons, the best response is to redo the meal **in correspondence to** their preferences. Although the food doesn't necessarily **meet up to** the chef's standard, but **pleasing** the customers and giving them **motivation** to come back is the secret for a successful restaurant.

# 中譯

若是廚師自己不懂烹調技巧，因此餐點遭到退回，便無可辯駁。但若是在烹調正確的情況下，仍然遭到抱怨時，該如何處置呢？以台灣餐飲為例，義大利餐館隨處可見。

在時下義大利麵、燉飯料理氾濫的情況下，大多數人仍不知道義大利餐點是以追求「彈牙」口感為特色，也就是米心、麵心稍微保有硬度的狀態。如此，在混合醬汁後，澱粉組織才不會呈現軟爛狀態。煮得道地、正統的義大利料理該是這樣的表現。然而，對華人來說，這樣乃是沒有煮透的狀態，也有人因此批評廚師不懂做菜。

因為不能強制要求客人對餐點了解得透徹，因此，若是客人因為自己的口味而將餐點退回，最好的方式，還是依照客人的偏好將餐點重新烹調過。儘管煮出來的料理不一定合乎廚師心目中的「最佳狀態」，但是如何取悅客人，並給與客人回訪的動力，才是一家餐廳經營的竅門。

# 字彙和慣用語一覽表

| | | | |
|---|---|---|---|
| elk | n. 麋鹿 | rubbery | adj. 橡膠般的 |
| guarantee | v. 擔保 | hold on to | 堅持 |
| preference | n. 偏好 | result in | 導致 |
| complaint | n. 抱怨 | rare | adj. 罕見的 |
| knowledgeable | adj. 知識淵博的 | texture | n. 口感 |
| grain | n. 穀物 | mushy | adj. 軟爛的 |
| average | adj. 平均的 | equal | v. 與…相等 |
| criticize | v. 批判 | be equipped with | 具有 |
| in correspondence to | 對應 | meet up to | 符合…的期望 |
| please | v. 討好 | motivation | n. 動機 |

Allen / 店員

Jeremy / 股東

 ## 情境對話

 MP3 49

**Jeremy :** Allen, did you just put the dishes in the dishwasher?

傑瑞米：艾倫，你剛剛是不是把盤子放到洗碗機裡去洗？

**Allen :** That's right. Is there a problem?

艾倫：是的，有什麼問題嗎？

**Jeremy :** You have to turn on the machine 30 minutes **ahead** of time to let the water **heat up**! You just used cold water for the dishes.

傑瑞米：你必須在使用前三十分鐘先打開熱機，水才會熱。你剛剛是用冷水洗盤子。

**Allen :** Oh no! Should I wash them again?

艾倫：噢不！我需要再洗一次嗎？

**Jeremy :** Of course you should! What a waste of water!

**Allen :** I'm sorry, boss.

**Jeremy :** By the way, did you put the **detergent** in the dish washer?

**Allen :** Hm…no.

**Jeremy :** From now on, you gotta remember how to use this machine, and make sure there is always detergent in the **storage**. If we run out of detergent during dinner service, we're **doomed**. You got me?

**Allen :** I'm sorry sir. I'll do exactly as you say.

傑瑞米：那還用說！真是浪費水！

艾倫：我很抱歉。

傑瑞米：還有，你有把洗碗精放到機器裡嗎？

艾倫：沒有。

傑瑞米：從現在起，你必須記得使用洗碗機的方法，還要確定庫存裡有洗碗精。如果晚餐時段洗碗精用完，我們就死定了！聽懂了沒？

艾倫：抱歉，我會照你說的辦。

# 哪裡有問題

因為艾倫是新進菜鳥,不知道洗碗機的使用方法,導致他用冷水洗碗,並且沒有使用洗碗機。雖然使用洗碗機聽起來很容易,但有些小細節還是需要注意。洗碗機的特點是使用熱水沖刷油汙,雖然各廠牌不同,但大部分都需先熱機,讓水升溫。在忙碌的供餐時段,迅速且確實的洗好碗盤、餐具很重要。通常負責洗碗的人只要搞懂使用方法,工作起來是相當順手輕鬆的。

# 餐飲補充包

Besides drinks-only coffee shops and bars, almost every restaurant has dishwashers. The size depends on the seats in the restaurant. In western countries, the **divisions** of work are clear in the kitchen. Usually, there is an employee who **specializes** in dish-washing. Operating the dishwasher is not **complicated**, yet problems during dining hours could cause a big trouble.

When the customers are many, plates get dirty fast. Dishwashers in popular restaurants are usually very busy. After all, running out of plates and glasses is **the last thing** one wants to encounter. When it happens, the dishwasher is the one to be **blamed**. Common **errors** of operating a dishwasher are: not **preheating** the water, **shortage** of detergent, **disarrangement** of the plates, etc. These reasons can result in washing dishes **in vain** and cause a waste of water.

**Apart from** learning how to use the machine, maintaining its **longevity** is also important. Big dishwashers are **pricy**, and a dishwasher employee should be aware of not putting **improper utensils** in the machine.

# 中譯

除了不供餐的咖啡廳或酒吧之外，絕大多數的餐廳都會配置洗碗機，大小依店面座位數而定。西方國家內場分工明確，通常洗碗會有專人負責。操作洗碗機不難，但若洗碗機在用餐時段出狀況，可能就會有大麻煩。

來客眾多時，餐盤消耗速度快，生意好的餐廳，洗碗工通常一刻都不得閒，畢竟沒盤子出餐、沒杯子出飲料是非常惱人的事，怪罪下來，責任無可推諉。操作洗碗機常見的錯誤有：未熱機就用冷水洗碗、沒有購置洗碗精、餐盤擺放錯誤等，種種原因都可能造成碗盤洗了等於沒洗，非常浪費水資源。

除了正確操作洗碗機之外，維持機器的壽命也是相當重要的。大型的洗碗機所費不貲，若擔任洗碗工，可要小心別把不該放進機器裡的東西放進去了。

# 字彙和慣用語一覽表

| | | | |
|---|---|---|---|
| ahead | adv. 在…之先 | heat up | 加溫 |
| detergent | n. 洗潔劑 | storage | n. 儲藏室 |
| doomed | adj. 註定的 | division | n. 分割 |
| specialize | v. 專門 | complicated | adj. 複雜的 |
| the last thing | 最不想…的事 | blame | v. 責備 |
| error | n. 錯誤 | preheat | v. 預熱 |
| storage | n. 儲存 | disarrangement | n. 混亂 |
| in vain | 白費功夫 | apart from | 除了…之外 |
| longevity | n. 壽命 | pricy | adj. 昂貴的 |
| improper | adj. 不適當的 | utensil | n. 用具 |

 Allen / 店員   Cathy / 廚師   Jeremy / 股東

 ## 情境對話

**Cathy :** Chicken roulade, **order up**!

凱西：雞肉捲做好了！

**Allen :** Cathy? Table ten says they ordered chicken roulade in bacon, not normal chicken roulade.

艾倫：凱西，十號桌説他們點的是培根雞肉捲，不是普通的雞肉捲喔。

**Cathy :** You serious? Gosh.

凱西：你認真的嗎？天哪。

**Jeremy :** Cathy, if you did the order wrong, **fix** it!

傑瑞米：凱西，如果妳做錯餐，就快點補救！

**Cathy :** I'm gonna. Sorry sir.

凱西：我會的，抱歉。

**Allen :** Are you going to make a new one? Should I tell them to wait?

艾倫：妳要做一份新的餐嗎？我需要請他們等嗎？

**Cathy :** Yeah. I'm making a new one right now.

凱西：需要。我立刻做一份新的。

**Jeremy :** Cathy, you gotta be **prudent** on this. Chicken roulade is **limited** every day, and you just wasted one dish!

傑瑞米：凱西，妳要謹慎一點。雞肉捲是每日限量的，妳剛剛就浪費了一份！

**Cathy :** I will **pay more attention** next time, sir.

凱西：下次我會注意的。

**Jeremy :** You better. That plate is your dinner tonight.

傑瑞米：那樣最好。今天妳的晚餐就是那盤。

**Allen :** Cathy, customer at Table ten says it's okay, he'd **rather** take this one **than** wait for another ten minutes.

艾倫：凱西，客人說沒關係，他寧願吃這盤雞肉捲，也不想再等十分鐘了。

**Cathy :** Awesome. Thank God!

凱西：太好了！感謝上天！

# 哪裡有問題

做錯餐點是廚房常見的狀況之一。雖然點單上寫得很清楚,但一忙起來,很容易就會看錯,有時候甚至因為忙到暈頭轉向,同一道菜重複做兩次都有可能。通常發生這種狀況,多出來的菜只能自行消化,不是變成員工餐就是倒掉。因此對話裡傑瑞米再三叫凱西多留意,畢竟多出來的開銷都是算在老闆頭上呢。

# 餐飲補充包

To cook food exactly and fast during rush hours is a big **challenge**. If the staff can **pull it**, the restaurant must be successful. In a kitchen, it is important to have a leader. Without **leadership**, it is difficult to work **precisely** and **efficiently** in the kitchen.

The head chef is usually the leader, yet sometimes the owner will take on the **task** himself. In western countries, it is common to ask for a customized meal in a restaurant, such as meat **doneness**, choices of side dishes, food being baked instead of fried, etc., situations **vary**. During rush hours, these **details** may **make a chef's head spin**.

If one dreams of working in the kitchen, apart from prudence and **concentration**, **obedience** to the leadership is also very important. If unfortunately, a wrong order is made, **according to** price of the ingredients, the **consequence** may not be too sweet.

# 中譯

在尖峰用餐時刻，廚房出餐準確且迅速是一大挑戰。若在這件事上掌握得宜，一間餐廳必然成功。廚房有人擔任領導地位是非常重要的；少了領導人物，廚房很難確實且有效率的分工。

通常首席廚師身負領導責任，有時則是由店東親自監督。歐美的餐廳常有客製化的服務，包括肉幾分熟、邊菜的選擇、甚至不要油炸改用烤的等等，各樣的狀況都可能出現，而在用餐尖峰時段，這些細節很可能讓廚師頭暈目眩。

若想在廚房工作，除了細心與專注之外，聽從主廚的指令也是非常重要的。若是做錯餐點，視食材價格，後果可不一定輕鬆喔！

# 字彙和慣用語一覽表

| | | | |
|---|---|---|---|
| order up | 上菜了 | fix | v. 修理 |
| prudent | adj. 謹慎的 | limited | adj. 限定的 |
| rather than | 而不是… | challenge | n. 挑戰 |
| pull it | （口）成功做到 | leadership | n. 領導地位 |
| precisely | adv. 精確地 | efficiently | adv. 有效率地 |
| task | n. 任務 | doneness | n. 熟度 |
| vary | v. 多變 | detail | n. 細節 |
| make sb. 's head spin | 使某人暈頭轉向 | concentration | n. 專注力 |
| obedience | n. 服從 | according to | 根據 |
| consequence | n. 後果 | | |

# Wrong Order 2
# 做錯餐點 2

 *Allen* / 店員　 *Cathy* / 廚師　 *Jeremy* / 股東

 情境對話

**Allen :** Cathy, the customer asked for medium, not medium-rare. They don't want to pay for it **unless** you make a new one.

**Cathy :** (murmur) Ridiculous.

**Jeremy :** Excuse me? That was your **fault**! If you can't **distinguish** medium meat and medium-rare meat, you can't stay in this kitchen.

艾倫：凱西，客人是點七分熟，不是五分熟。他們說如果妳不重做一份新的，他們就不付錢。

凱西：（自言自語）荒唐。

傑瑞米：我有沒有聽錯呀？那是妳的錯！如果妳不知道七分熟和五分熟之間的差別，妳就不該待在廚房！

**Cathy :** I'm sorry Jeremy, I know it's a huge mistake. It's my fault.

凱西：抱歉，傑瑞米，我知道這是大問題。是我的錯。

**Allen :** Also, the duck breast is overdone. The customer said he required pink and tender duck breast, not a tough and dry piece of meat.

艾倫：還有，鴨胸煮過頭了。客人說他要的是帶粉紅又柔軟的鴨胸，而不是一塊又硬又乾的肉。

**Jeremy :** Cathy, **what's got into you** today? You always **execute** perfectly. **Perform**! Come on, girl.

傑瑞米：凱西，妳今天是怎麼了？平常妳都表現得很好呀。拜託妳振作一點！

**Cathy :** I guess the **overwhelming** tickets **are getting the best of me**. I'll **start over** again.

凱西：我想今天的點單真的多到讓我不能負荷了。我會重作的。

**Jeremy :** Today you're **off the hook**, but next time you won't **get away with it**. Help me out here, okay?

傑瑞米：今天我就不追究了，下次可沒這麼容易。妳也幫幫忙嘛。

# 哪裡有問題

第二種做錯餐點的問題，是食物的烹調程度不如預期。
在台灣，通常要在較高檔的餐廳，才能就此問題對廚房
提出抗議，但在歐美的餐廳卻很常見。

對話中，客人因不滿意牛排和鴨胸，而將菜餚退回廚
房。好在牛排還能補救，但鴨胸就只能丟棄了。

發生這種事，老闆絕對不會高興。若不是受過專業訓練
的廚師，要在廚房工作，平常最好多練習肉類料理。

# 餐飲補充包

The doneness of the meat is **sacred** in western cuisine. If a customer asks for certain doneness and it is not fulfilled, it can raise **severe** protests. The doneness of a steak can be **categorized** by rare, medium-rare, medium, and well-done. The most common one is medium-rare steak, which is pink in the middle with a brown crust around it, and no blood **leaking**.

Well-done steak is hardly required. If a steak is too raw, it can still be **restored**, while a well-done steak is cooked-to-death and must be started over. Other common meats are duck breast, chicken breast, pork chop, and lamb chop. Although these ones are not categorized by doneness, they can be overcooked easily. Overcooked meat is tough and dry; it's very hard to eat. If the meal gets returned, it has to be started **from scratch**.

For a restaurant, starting over a dish like this is time-consuming and expensive; for a cook, it's embarrassing. Even if the owner doesn't ask for the money, it hurts one's **reputation** as a cook. **For your own good**, better watch out in the kitchen.

# 中譯

肉的熟度在西餐的領域中是相當神聖的,若是客人要求特定熟度,未達標準可是會被強烈抗議的。牛排的熟度一般而言分為三分熟、五分熟、七分熟、全熟,最常見的是五分熟,也就是肉切開中間是粉紅色,但沒有血水流出的狀態;全熟的牛排較少人要求。

通常煮得太生還能補救,煮到全熟就回天乏術了,只能重新再做。其他常見的肉還有鴨胸、雞胸、豬排、羊排等。這些肉雖不像牛排分許多熟度,卻非常容易煮得過老。烹調過頭的肉通常又硬又乾,很難入口,這時候若被退貨,就只能認栽重來。

對餐廳而言,排餐被要求重作是耗時又傷本的事,對負責的廚師而言更是相當難堪。即使老闆不一定會要廚師賠錢,但這對自身名譽很傷,所以還是多加留心為上。

# 字彙和慣用語一覽表

| | | | |
|---|---|---|---|
| unless | 除非 | murmur | v. 咕噥 |
| fault | n. 過失 | distinguish | v. 分辨 |
| what's that into sb. | 某人是怎麼了 | execute | v. 執行 |
| perform | v. 表現 | overwhelming | adj. 壓倒性的 |
| get the best of sb. | 著了…的道 | start over | 重新開始 |
| off the hook | 放某人一馬 | get away with it | 逃過一劫 |
| sacred | adj. 神聖的 | severe | adj. 嚴重的 |
| categorize | v. 分類 | leak | v. 漏 |
| restore | v. 恢復 | from scratch | 從頭開始 |
| reputation | n. 名聲 | for sb. 's own good | 為了某人好 |

# Too Slow
# 出餐過慢

*Allen* / 店員　　*Cathy* / 廚師　　*Jeremy* / 股東

 ## 情境對話

MP3 52

**Jeremy :** Cathy, Table eight and Table twelve have been waiting for half an hour. Can I get their entrées please?

傑瑞米：凱西，八桌和十二桌已經等半小時了。可以把他們的餐給我嗎？

**Cathy :** I'm doing it. The burger takes ten minutes to cook, and they ordered eight burgers! I can only do so much **at one time**.

凱西：我已經在做了。漢堡肉煮熟要花十分鐘，而他們點了八個堡！我一次能做的事有限。

**Jeremy : At least** give me something! Is it that hard?

傑瑞米：至少給我點什麼吧！有那麼難？

**Cathy :** Alright. Here's two burgers.

凱西：兩個漢堡做好了。

**Allen :** Here's your burger. Sorry to keep you waiting.

艾倫：這是您的漢堡。抱歉讓您久等了。

**Customer :** That's okay. Good food is **worth** the wait.

客人：沒關係，美味值得等待。

**Allen :** Thank you. That's very kind of you.

艾倫：謝謝您的體諒。

**Jeremy :** Allen, give some pretzels to those who haven't received food yet. Don't let them feel **bored**. Cathy, you need to get things **organized**. If there are too many of the same order, you have to choose a **priority**. Don't make everything at once. It's **killing me**.

傑瑞米：艾倫，拿些扭結鹹餅乾給還未上菜的客人。別讓他們覺得無聊。凱西，妳要有系統一點。如果同時太多相同的料理要做，要分優先順序，不要全部同時做。我快緊張死啦。

**Cathy :** I'm sorry. I won't do it again.

凱西：抱歉，我不會再這樣了。

 # 哪裡有問題

對話中，凱西因無法同時料理好八個漢堡，造成客人久等。

對廚師來說，料理餐點的順序，必須在接到點單的幾秒內決定，而這個決定會直接影響客人拿到料理的時間點。

通常若同時料理好幾道相同的菜餚，因廚房空間的限制，客人勢必會等得較久。這時可選擇先出一兩道餐，不一定要全部做好同時出，或是先招待小點心，讓客人可以墊墊肚子。

# 餐飲補充包

Maintaining a certain **pace** in food serving is a key to the restaurant business. Making fresh food **to order**, yet not taking too long for food to arrive at the customers' table, is a **task** for both the cook and the owner.

Normally, as soon as the ticket arrives, the cooks start to prepare the dish. However, different dish requires different amount of time. For instance, a risotto takes at least 25 minutes, while angel hair pasta only takes 10 minutes. As a result, if a customer arrives earlier, he doesn't **necessarily** get the food faster. In order to have a better **understanding**, the servers are supposed to **inform** customers of the time each dish takes, and make sure everyone is **on the same page**.

Nevertheless, if too many customers **pour in** at the same time, it's more **likely** that the kitchen will be **buried** in tickets. At this moment, the cook must have a clear head to complete every dish correctly. In the **chaotic craziness**, the **cooperation** of cooks and servers is what leads to a good pace of food serving.

# 中譯

維持一定的出餐速度是經營餐廳的重要關鍵。如何在接到點單後烹調新鮮食材，卻不至於讓客人等到肚子大叫空城，是廚師和業主的共同課題。

通常在外場接到點單後，廚房會立即開始料理食物，然而不同的食材料理時間長短不同，例如燉飯至少要二十五分鐘、天使髮義大利麵卻只要十分鐘。因此，並非先到的顧客就一定會先拿到食物。為避免客人心理不平衡，侍者在點餐時最好先說明那些料理需要久候，並在取得客人的理解後再行點餐。

然而，若同時間湧入太多客人，廚房可能會被點單淹沒，這時候廚師的思路就必須夠清晰，才能按部就班地完成料理。在一片忙碌的混亂中，若廚師和侍者有默契，出餐速度較能維持穩定。

# 字彙和慣用語一覽表

| | | | |
|---|---|---|---|
| at one time | 一次 | at least | 至少 |
| worth | adj. 值得的 | bored | adj. 感到無聊的 |
| organized | adj. 有組織的 | priority | n. 優先順序 |
| sth. is killing sb. | 某事使人難受 | pace | n. 速度 |
| to order | 訂購 | task | n. 任務 |
| necessarily | adv. 必定 | understanding | n. 理解 |
| inform | v. 告知 | on the same page | 有共識 |
| pour in | 湧入 | likely | adj. 可能的 |
| bury | v. 埋 | chaotic | adj. 混亂的 |
| craziness | n. 瘋狂 | cooperation | n. 合作 |

# Cut Oneself
# 切到自己

*Allen* / 店員

*Cathy* / 廚師

*Jeremy* / 股東

 **情境對話**

MP3
53

**Cathy :** Allen, after you finish peeling the potatoes, I need you to peel the carrots and cut the Napa cabbage.

**凱西：**艾倫，你削完馬鈴薯後，我需要你幫忙削胡蘿蔔和切大白菜。

**Allen :** Ouch!

**艾倫：**唉唷！

**Cathy :** What's going on? You cut yourself?

**凱西：**發生什麼事了？你切到手了嗎？

**Allen :** Unfortunately, yes.

**艾倫：**很不幸的，正是如此。

**Cathy :** Stop whatever you're doing, and go to the

**凱西：**停下你手邊的工作，趕快去洗手台洗手。

sink.

**Allen :** I guess I'm actually okay, Cathy. Not a deep cut.

**Jeremy :** Listen to Cathy, kid. Do you know what will happen if the customers find out that there's blood in our food?

**Allen :** Hm…disgusted, I suppose?

**Jeremy :** It's **bacteria**, for Christ's sake! It's **contamination**! That can bring us a lawsuit and we can **go belly-up**! That's no joke!

**Allen :** Wow. I'd better take care of my **wound** then.

**Cathy :** Now you know why we always have Vaseline and Band-Aids on the kitchen shelf.

艾倫：我覺得應該還好，切得不深。

傑瑞米：聽凱西的話，小子。你知道如果客人發現他們食物裡有血液，會有什麼後果嗎？

艾倫：呃…可能會覺得噁心吧？

傑瑞米：是細菌，老天！這是細菌汙染！這會害我們被告，餐廳可能會關門大吉！這可不是開玩笑。

艾倫：哇，我最好妥善處理我的傷口了。

凱西：現在你知道為什麼廚房架子上都要放凡士林和OK繃了吧。

# 哪裡有問題

對話中，艾倫切到手卻認爲沒有大礙，想要不處理就繼
續工作，結果被傑瑞米念了一頓。食品安全在餐飲業裡
是很重要的一環，不潔的食物會造成嚴重的後果，甚至
導致餐廳關門。因此，不管傷口再小，都必須先處理乾
淨，並確保不會影響菜餚後才能繼續工作。這是疏忽不
得的事，畢竟沒有人希望自己的餐盤裡有不知名的血液
吧！

# 餐飲補充包

Kitchen hygiene is **extremely** important. Besides a clean environment, the cooks **bear** most of the responsibility. An **ill** cook is supposed to call in sick to prevent **germs** and contamination. He or she shouldn't continue working under ill conditions. **In addition**, to avoid fallen hairs, usually a hat is required in the kitchen, and women are asked to tie their hair.

It's common to cut oneself in the kitchen, however, the emergency **treatment** is **ignored** in many cases. Knives, peelers and graters can cause serious bleeding. It's important to put the wound under running water immediately, and make sure it's cleaned **thoroughly**. Then comes **disinfection**, medicine and a Band-Aid. Finally, a pair of **antibacterial** gloves and the work can **carry on**. If the cut is too deep, the **individual** should be taken to the hospital.

In **formal** culinary **competitions**, a chef that cuts himself or herself is usually **eliminated automatically**. The importance is seen thusly. Food hygiene is not only about the health of the customers, but also the reputation of a restaurant.

## 中譯

廚房衛生是非常重要的事，除了環境維持整潔外，廚師本身也身負重任。為避免細菌感染，廚師若身體不適便應告假，不能勉強工作以免汙染食物。另外，為避免毛髮等汙染，工作中通常會佩戴帽子，女性則被要求挽起頭髮。

廚房中切到手是家常便飯，然而傷處的處理卻常被輕忽。刀具、削皮器或刨刀都可能造成大量出血，此時須立刻將傷處以流水沖洗，確保傷處的清潔。之後進行消毒、擦藥並包上OK 繃，最後帶上抗菌手套後才能繼續工作。若傷口過深，則必須就醫。

在正式的餐飲類競賽中，若廚師受傷，通常會立刻失去比賽資格，可見食物衛生的重要性。傷處的細菌及人體內自存的疾病等都可能藉由血液傳播，因此不可不慎。食物的衛生不僅關乎客人的健康，更是餐廳信譽的表現。

# 字彙和慣用語一覽表

| bacteria | n. 細菌 | contamination | n. 汙染 |
|---|---|---|---|
| go belly-up | 倒閉 | wound | n. 傷口 |
| extremely | adv. 極度地 | bear | v. 承擔 |
| ill | adj. 生病的 | germ | n. 病菌 |
| in addition | 除此之外 | treatment | n. 治療 |
| ignore | v. 忽略 | thoroughly | adv. 徹底地 |
| disinfection | n. 消毒 | antibacterial | adj. 抗菌的 |
| carry on | 繼續 | individual | n. 個人 |
| formal | adj. 正式的 | competition | n. 競賽 |
| eliminate | v. 淘汰 | automatically | adv. 自動地 |

# Prepped Food Problems
# 食材處理有誤

 Allen / 店員　 Cathy / 廚師　 Jeremy / 股東

 **情境對話**

**Cathy :** I only see a **darn bucket**. You didn't **marinate** them in buttermilk?

凱西：我只看到一個籃子。你沒用發酵奶醃雞肉嗎？

**Allen :** I.... It must have **slipped my mind**.

艾倫：我…我想我忘記了。

**Cathy :** You can't be serious. Also, where are the baby spinach that I'm planning to use as a side?

凱西：你在開玩笑。那，今天要當配菜的幼菠菜呢？

**Allen :** They are still in the bag...

艾倫：還在袋子裡…

**Cathy :** Why is nothing ready?

**Jeremy :** Allen, did you come in at 10 am or did you **oversleep**?

**Allen :** I overslept sir. I'm sorry, Cathy.

**Jeremy :** Boy, listen to me, if you want to stay here, do as I say. Follow Cathy's **instructions**, and no more late night parties.

**Allen :** Understood. Cathy, where should I start?

**Cathy :** Well, there's nothing you can do about the chicken. Why don't you go ahead and start washing the vegetables?

**Allen : You got it**.

凱西：為什麼沒有一件事做完？

傑瑞米：艾倫，你是早上十點就來，還是你睡過頭？

艾倫：我睡過頭了。抱歉，凱西。

傑瑞米：小子，你聽好，如果你還想在這裡混的話，最好照我說的做。凱西說的話你要好好聽，然後不准再跑趴玩通宵了。

艾倫：知道了。凱西，我該從哪裡開始？

凱西：雞肉的話是幫不上忙了，你去洗菜吧。

艾倫：了解。

 # 哪裡有問題

通常餐廳在開始營業前，會提前四、五小時處理食材，確保各種食材到位，好避免在忙碌的節骨眼上做洗菜、切肉之類的小事。這些事前的處理相當重要，特別像醃肉這類需要時間的備料手續，相當影響料理的美味度。對話中，艾倫忘了用發酵奶醃雞肉，將會造成雞肉不夠軟嫩多汁，這可能導致老闆決定當天不銷售該道料理。

# 餐飲補充包

In a restaurant, usually food is prepared in the morning or the night before. There is so much to do before the door opens to the customers.

Meat needs to be properly **portioned** and cut, the vegetables need to be **trimmed** and washed, **just to name a few** jobs. In some big restaurants, there are people working in the morning just to get every ingredient done and done right.

It is called a prep cook. They prepare the **broth**, which is the **soul** for every good dish, marinate the meat, **keep** vegetables **in good shape**, roll out pasta, **form** the meatballs, etc. Prep work is just as important as cooking itself, and it's **crucial** that the owner has everything **on track**.

It is no fun **running out of** ingredients **in the middle of** dinner service, and it's as **dreadful** as hell to have to cut your chops while the tickets are **flooding** in.

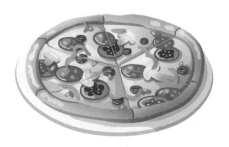

# 中譯

通常餐廳的食材都會在早晨或前一天晚上準備好，在餐廳的大門向客人敞開前，有太多事需要安排了。

肉類需要適當分配並切塊，蔬菜類需要修剪、清洗，諸如此類。在一些規模比較大的餐廳，有些人在早上專門處理這些食材，他們被稱為預餐廚師。

這些廚師烹煮高湯，高湯是每道好菜的靈魂；醃肉、處理蔬菜、製作義大利麵、手打肉丸…等等。前置作業跟烹煮的過程同等重要，對一家餐廳的老闆來說，對每樣食材的庫存了然於胸是必須的。

在上餐期間發生食材不足的問題不是開玩笑，而在點單如雪花般飛進廚房時，還必須現切豬排同樣是一件令人害怕的事。

# 字彙和慣用語一覽表

| | | | |
|---|---|---|---|
| darn | damn 的委婉說法 | bucket | n. 桶子 |
| marinate | v. 醃漬 | slip out of one's head | 忘記 |
| oversleep | v. 睡過頭 | instruction | n. 指令 |
| you got it | 知道了、明白了 | portion | v. 分配 |
| trim | v. 修剪 | just to name a few | 僅列舉幾個 |
| broth | n. 高湯 | soul | n. 靈魂 |
| keep…in good shape | 使…有好的狀態 | form | v. 使成形 |
| crucial | adj. 重要的 | on track | 保持追蹤 |
| run out of | 用完… | in the middle of | 在…之中 |
| dreadful | adj. 可怕的 | flood | v. 淹水 |

**Learn Smart 076**

## 餐飲人邁向國際的必備關鍵口說英語（附 MP3）

| | |
|---|---|
| 作　　　者 | 陳怡歆 |
| 發 行 人 | 周瑞德 |
| 執行總監 | 齊心瑀 |
| 行銷經理 | 楊景輝 |
| 企劃編輯 | 陳韋佑 |
| 封面構成 | 高鍾琪 |

| | |
|---|---|
| 內頁構成 | 菩薩蠻數位文化有限公司 |
| 印　　　製 | 大亞彩色印刷製版股份有限公司 |
| 初　　　版 | 2017 年 3 月 |
| 定　　　價 | 新台幣 380 元 |
| 出　　　版 | 倍斯特出版事業有限公司 |
| 電　　　話 | (02) 2351-2007 |
| 傳　　　真 | (02) 2351-0887 |
| 地　　　址 | 100 台北市中正區福州街 1 號 10 樓之 2 |
| E - m a i l | best.books.service@gmail.com |
| 網　　　址 | www.bestbookstw.com |

| | |
|---|---|
| 港澳地區總經銷 | 泛華發行代理有限公司 |
| 地　　　址 | 香港新界將軍澳工業邨駿昌街 7 號 2 樓 |
| 電　　　話 | (852) 2798-2323 |
| 傳　　　真 | (852) 2796-5471 |

**國家圖書館出版品預行編目資料**

餐飲人邁向國際的必備關鍵口說英語
／ 陳怡歆著. -- 初版. -- 臺北市 :
倍斯特, 2017.03 面 ; 公分. --
(Learn smart ;
76)ISBN978-986-93766-9-3( 平裝附
光碟片 )
1.英語 2.餐飲業 3.會話
　805.188　　　　　　106001670